Best Friends & Their Exes

Zoë Tavares Bennett

MEDITERRA
PRESS

To everyone who supported my debut novel. Thank you for believing in me.

And to my sister, who is still and forever shall be my best friend.

Contents

1

"**A**re you sure you don't want to come with us?" Jenny asked.

Aspen looked up at Jenny and tried to smile. "I'm busy, but maybe next week."

"You say that every time," Jenny said with a sigh. "But your call."

Her other colleagues said their goodbyes and began filing out of the studio. Jenny flipped her bleach blonde hair behind her shoulder and walked out the door with the rest of the model agency staff. Except Aspen.

"I'll close up," Aspen called after them, even though they already knew she would.

Once they were all out the door, Aspen sighed, running a hand through her hair. She itched to get out her phone and text Vera, to ask her to come over or something since it was a Friday night. But she knew Vera wouldn't answer, and even if she did, she would say that she was studying and didn't want any distractions. That's all Aspen was to her now—a distraction.

Her time so far in Los Angeles hadn't been what she expected. She had thought they would take on the glitz and glam together, holding hands and daring anyone to judge them for it. Aspen had thought she would be a famous model by now and Vera would study at UCLA and they would have fun together at college parties.

Instead, Aspen was a struggling model, working an underpaid assistant job at an agency to pay the rent for her expensive apartment, while Vera studied at UCLA and never had time for her. Aspen didn't blame Vera for studying a lot and caring about her grades. But even when she wasn't in class or preparing for a big exam, if Aspen asked whether she wanted to come over, Vera claimed she was too tired, or that she was meeting with a classmate to study, or she had to visit her family. There was always an excuse.

Aspen hadn't brought up her concerns with Vera yet because she was scared of losing her again. The first time was horrible, even though it wasn't technically a breakup. At the beginning of her senior year, they 'took time off' because Vera's schedule was too busy, what with adjusting to UCLA's heavy workload and the long distance putting a strain on their relationship. In other words, they were breaking up. Aspen had cried for three days straight after that and had missed a week of school.

The rest of senior year was miserable. Aspen tried to be happy, to think of the good things in her life, like her dad being cancer-free and the family adopting another dog, but it just wasn't the same. Layla had even suggested seeing a therapist.

And then the summer came, Vera along with it. They started hanging out again, and soon enough they were back to where they started a year ago. At the time, Aspen had been excited and hopeful about the upcoming year, about living in Los Angeles and sharing an apartment with Vera.

But two months into the Fall semester, Aspen realized that things had changed. Instead of sharing an apartment together, Vera had opted to live in UCLA housing with her freshman-year roommate, claiming that it was cheaper and more convenient, despite the fact that she had always complained about the small rooms and her roommate's messy habits. Though she promised that they would move in together next year, Vera was completely engrossed in her studies and her engineering friends, and she seemed to be losing interest in Aspen as well.

Now Aspen was just waiting for Vera to finally end it.

After thirty minutes of driving solemnly from the agency, Aspen arrived at her apartment. She tried not to think too hard about the loneliness she felt upon being greeted by darkness, with no signs of life save for her pet fish on the side table.

It was almost ten o'clock at night, so she decided to text Vera.

Aspen: *Have a good day?*

Aspen was surprised when Vera answered a few seconds later.

Vera: *Not really…*

Aspen: *Want me to come over?*

Vera: *Only if you want to.*

Aspen stared at her screen in shock. This must've been the first time in weeks that Vera let her come over to her dorm. Her hands trembled as she typed a reply.

Aspen: *Be there in ten.*

She grabbed her keys again and jogged outside. It was hard not to speed, but Aspen restrained herself so that she wouldn't risk a speeding ticket. After ten long minutes, she finally reached UCLA and entered the parking lot near Vera's dorm. It was at least a two-minute walk, but she didn't mind as long as she got to see Vera.

The door to the dorm lobby opened, revealing Vera's familiar red glasses and frizzy, brown hair that she had always found endearing. Aspen could tell how exhausted she was in her lackluster smile.

"Hey," Vera said quietly as she opened the door wider for Aspen to come inside.

Aspen took her hand and kissed her briefly. "It's good to see you."

Vera averted her eyes and led them to her dorm room on the first floor. "My roommate isn't here yet."

They silently entered her dorm room, a small space hardly wide enough to have two twin beds placed on either side. Vera's roommate was messy and her bed was covered in dirty laundry and textbooks. Vera's side, on the other hand, was impeccable, her bed made with a pastel striped duvet and her books neatly stacked on her desk.

Aspen laced their hands together as they sat on the edge of the small bed. "So tell me. What's going on?"

"I'm just exhausted," Vera said, looking at her lap, "and I haven't had more than ten hours of sleep this entire week."

Aspen inspected Vera more closely and was mildly horrified at the dark smudges under Vera's eyes, the cracked lips, and the paleness of her complexion. "That's awful! You won't be able to survive the whole year if you keep that up. You shouldn't have so much work to do that you can't get at least four or five hours of sleep a night. It's inhumane."

Vera pulled her hand away to fix her glasses and smooth down her hair. "I would be able to get more hours of sleep if my dorm building ever slept at night. All they do is party and play loud music. Even if I do get work done early, I can never fall asleep. Like, don't they have lives?"

Aspen didn't hesitate. "You can move in with me," she offered, trying to tone down her excitement. Vera immediately shrunk away from her, like Aspen knew she would, avoiding Aspen's eyes.

"I don't know—"

"But I know," Aspen interrupted.

Vera picked at the threads of the mattress. "I think—"

"Don't think."

"But—" Vera started.

"What are you so scared of?"

Vera exhaled, clearly vexed. "Aspen…"

Aspen groaned. "It would be perfect! You'd have a quiet place to work, and UCLA is only ten minutes away. And on the weekends we could go to parties if you were free or spend all day inside if we wanted."

But Vera looked unconvinced. "That's a little…fast, don't you think?"

"Vera, we've been together for almost two years," Aspen said, watching as Vera blushed and turned away uncomfortably. "Wait, you're not worried about...the intimacy part, are you? Because I feel like we've covered a fair share of ground on that front."

Vera blushed a darker shade of red. "No."

"Then what is it? I just don't get it. Do you even like me anymore?" Aspen was only half-serious, but Vera's head shot up, and the sparkling guilt in her eyes was answer enough. Aspen stood up from the bed, her face hot with embarrassment.

"I should go," Aspen said, numbly heading toward the door. "Clearly you don't even want to be with me."

"Aspen, wait," Vera said warily. Aspen paused with her hand on the doorknob. "I didn't say that. But aren't you worried it's not going to work out? You're busy with modeling, I'm busy with school. Maybe it's not meant to be. We tried to make it work but..."

"But that's life, Vera," Aspen said angrily, turning around. "We'll always be busy. *You're* the one who never makes the time for us anymore. I never go to parties with my colleagues because of us. I live alone in my sad, dark apartment because of you. We never do any fun things because *you* always have an excuse."

Vera's eyes filled with tears as Aspen spoke, but she found it hard to care when Vera was the one who was having doubts in the first place. "Well, maybe you *should* go party with your model friends. Maybe that way you'll find a hotter replacement for me and you can finally have all the fun you want without me dampening your mood."

"Oh, that's rich coming from you. You're the one who constantly hangs out with your engineering friends instead of your girlfriend! Am I not smart enough for you or something?"

Before Vera could answer, the door swung open. Vera's roommate walked inside, eyeing Vera and Aspen curiously as she dumped her backpack on her desk and crawled into her bed, immediately scrolling on her phone.

"You should go," Vera said quietly, remaining on the bed, a tear sliding down her cheek. "I have class early tomorrow morning."

Aspen hesitated, but when she saw Vera's stiff posture and the resolution in her eyes, she knew the argument would go nowhere. She practically ran back to her car, and only once she entered her apartment did she allow herself to collapse on her bed and cry.

When her tears subsided, Aspen grabbed her phone. Vera hadn't even tried to text or call. Aspen dialed the number of the one person whom she could talk with, who understood how much Vera meant to her.

"Aspen?" Layla said when the line connected. Aspen

hiccuped before she could say anything. "Aspen, what's wrong?"

The tears started to fall rapidly again. Her voice was thick and wavering when she said, "It's over."

Layla sucked in a breath on the other end of the line. "Are you—did she end it?"

Aspen sobbed again, louder and more pitiful. "B-basically."

"But what did she say?" Layla pressed.

"She said…she said that I should go party with my model friends, that we tried to make it work but we're too busy," Aspen said, then took in a deep breath. "I don't want to talk about it."

"Okay, you don't have to. I'll talk with her," Layla said hurriedly. "It'll be alright, Aspen. I promise."

But Aspen didn't believe her. Because without Vera, her life was empty and pointless. Nothing could ever be alright again.

2

"How do I look?" Layla asked, twirling in the mirror and watching her long black skirt swish around her legs. She had taken to wearing darker clothes since moving to New York City, and her friends at fashion school had encouraged her to try out new styles.

Her boyfriend, Zach, glanced up from his phone and squinted at her across the room. She had stayed the night at his apartment, which his parents were renting for him. "If you're going for sexy nun, then you look great."

Layla frowned at her skirt paired with a cropped black sweater. "I don't look like a nun. Nuns would never show their stomachs."

"I'm joking babe, you look hot as always," Zach said with a laugh, swinging his legs off the bed and standing up. He stretched his arms out with a yawn, scratching at his dark brown hair which was still messy from sleep. "When are you done with class?"

"Not until five," Layla said, shrieking when Zach suddenly came up behind her and barreled her in a hug. "Get off me!"

He kissed her neck, ignoring her fake protests. "Mmm…wanna meet me at the studio? We can go for dinner after today's recording session."

Layla hesitated. Zach was the lead guitarist in a minor indie band called *Red Head.* They worked at the studio for several hours a day, usually staying well past dinner and leaving her hungry and annoyed. But that wasn't the only reason she disliked visiting his studio. Besides, she still had to call Vera and ask about the Aspen situation, then call Aspen about the Vera situation.

"We'll go to your favorite sushi restaurant," Zach offered. "On me. Come on babe, you know I love it when you're in the studio. And it's Friday, so you don't have school tomorrow."

"Fine," Layla relented. "Now get off me or I'll be late for class!"

She managed to extract herself from Zach's arms after a few pacifying kisses and hurried off to her first class of the day, which was on the west side of the city from his apartment.

When she exited the lobby doors of the apartment building, she was immediately enveloped in Manhattan's bustling morning rush. Cars honked and sped past the busy intersection as she crossed the street towards the subway station. Zach's apartment was in the East Village, so it would take her almost thirty minutes on the subway to get to her campus in Chelsea, where the Fashion Institute of Technology was located.

She slipped in earbuds as she boarded the L train, which was too crowded to find a seat. Taylor Swift's new album drowned out the screeching of the subway cars and the chatter of commuters.

After switching to the E train, the subway cart soon shuddered to a stop at 23rd Street. Layla secured her tote bag over her shoulder and hurriedly walked the three long blocks to her first class on Stretch Fundamentals, which included an hour-long lecture, a small break for coffee and food, and then a three-hour lab.

Layla could not help but smile as she wove through the crowds of people on the sidewalk, despite the sun shining bleakly through the clouds and the startling chill of late October mornings that she still had not gotten used to. She loved New York City—the pace, the smells, the noise, all of it so foreign to the sleepy, sunny suburbia she was used to in Southern California. Although she often missed the warmth of the sun and her spontaneous trips to the beach, here in the city she felt as though all her dreams of entering the fashion world and falling in love were coming true.

Her lecture class was on the fifth floor of a large brick building faced with beautiful stone trimming. Layla was nearly late but found her seat in the back rows of the classroom before the professor began lecturing on fine gauge knits.

The day sped on with the amount of information she struggled to cram into her notebook, since she refused to type notes on her computer. She laughed and gossiped with her friends at the break as they crossed the street for a bagel and coffee before returning to their lab.

It was almost sunset when she left the lab and caught a subway to the studio where Zach recorded with his band. They had been an official band since Zach was a freshman in college at NYU, which was four years ago. During the summer before his senior year, his band blew up on social media and they decided to drop out to pursue music more seriously. It helped that Zach's parents had money to spare in order to support his endeavors.

Layla had met him at a party early in September where his band was playing, and even from the dance floor, he had caught her eye. He had deft fingers that skillfully played the guitar and thick, chocolate-brown hair that fell in careless strands over a sharp brow. That night he bought her a drink and by the end of the month they were dating. It had all happened so fast that Layla hardly had time to think about it, her flashy new life of concerts, after-parties, and fashion school burying any doubts she had about their whirlwind romance.

Luckily Zach's studio was near her campus on the top floor with a beautiful view of the Flat Iron building and the skyline of the city. She took the elevator up, her stomach already twisting into knots. The studio had always intimidated her.

The elevator deposited her in the dark hallway of the main studios. She could hear voices from the room that Zach usually played in. Before she reached the door, it opened, and Gianna, the beautiful redheaded lead singer—and inspiration behind the band's name—sauntered out in her high heels.

"Oh hey," she said in her deep, melodic voice as she approached. "Zach just started recording."

Then Gianna walked past her and through a door on the other side of the hall that led to the kitchen, where the studio kept refreshments for their artists. Layla barely said hello back before Gianna's long red curls swished behind the door and disappeared.

Layla took a deep breath in, trying to cool the indignation she always felt towards Zach's band members, who were on the surface infuriatingly nice, though Layla still detected an underlying amusement, or even condescension, towards her, as if they pitied her for being Zach's new girlfriend. She knew that Zach was notorious among his band members for his tumultuous dating history, but they didn't need to project his past on their future together.

After all, she wasn't naive. Zach was older, more experienced, and semi-famous. She didn't expect them to get married or anything. At least, not when she thought about it logically. This was about having fun in college, not long, lasting commitments. Still, she couldn't help that twinge of jealousy when she saw the flocks of beautiful girls crowding the stages at their concerts or that inevitable moment during a song when Gianna made smoldering eye contact with Zach as he shredded a solo on his guitar.

Inside the studio was dark and illuminated with mood lighting. On one side of the glass were Zach's songwriters and studio manager, along with his other band members, Serenity on bass and Mateo on the drums. On the other side of the glass stood Zach with his guitar, frowning in concentration as he played into the mike.

She waved silently to Serenity and Mateo, who nodded at her with small, polite smiles as she took a seat and watched Zach pluck the guitar strings with expert speed. Since the sound could only be heard through the headphones that the others were wearing, Layla sat in an awkward silence.

A few moments later, Gianna walked back inside, passing Layla to grab the last pair of headphones on the main desk. She glanced at Layla as if she were an afterthought and gestured to the headphones in her hand.

"Do you want to listen?" she asked in her casual, effortless way.

Layla shook her head quickly. "Oh, no thanks. You should listen."

Gianna merely shrugged a slim shoulder and slipped the headphones on, and soon she was nodding her head to the beat of the music. The others seemed similarly engrossed in Zach's guitar solo and paid her little mind, so she took out her phone and scrolled through social media.

It felt like hours passed when he finished, though she checked the time and it had only been about fifteen minutes. Suddenly the others began clapping and Layla looked up. Zach was grinning on the other side of the glass. He caught her eye and nodded his head at her, before quickly focusing his attention on his bandmates. Layla tried not to feel silly, knowing that he was in the middle of a recording session and needed to remain focused on his work.

"That was some good stuff, Zach!" exclaimed the studio manager—either Jeremy or James, Layla always forgot—once Zach exited the studio chamber.

"Thanks, man," Zach said, shaking his manager's hand. "I think that's all I have in me today. I promised Layla dinner tonight. We're getting sushi."

The others all looked at her. Layla fought a hot blush on her cheeks, though she didn't know why she was so embarrassed. She felt vaguely like an annoying younger sister that Zach had to babysit.

"Ooh, I love sushi!" Serenity said. "Do you mind if I tag along?"

"And me?" Gianna asked as she packed up her belongings. "Mateo and I were already going to dinner."

Layla felt her heart pound in dread. She glanced at Zach, but he only raised a brow, as if it were up to her.

"You guys can come," she said quietly, struggling to smile.

Zach grinned. "It's a party!"

Serenity slung an arm around Zach affectionately like a sister might and walked out of the studio with him. Gianna laughed and joined them, jumping into a conversation about his solo recording session. Layla let them pass her, pretending to fiddle with her tote bag and phone.

"Are you good?" Mateo asked in his soft Brazilian accent, eyeing her knowingly. Out of everyone, he seemed to be the most sensitive to her feelings. Perhaps this was because he understood all too well what it was like to feel left out.

"Yes, thank you. Just tired from a long day."

Mateo nodded, unconvinced, but he didn't press her. "Nothing a shot of Sake won't fix."

Layla sighed. "I guess you're right."

The studio manager laughed. "Better get used to it, darling! It's a full-time job to date a music star. Think of his band as your in-laws."

Mateo rolled his eyes. "Come on. They're probably already downstairs."

She left the studio and together they walked out to the elevators. Mateo pressed the down button, and the ding of the elevator's arrival sounded like a warning bell in her stomach.

"I'm gonna go to the restroom," Layla said suddenly. "You go down without me. Tell Zach I'll be there in a minute."

Mateo nodded silently, then slipped into the elevator when the doors opened.

Layla let out a long breath once he disappeared. She needed a moment alone before she was consumed by the band for the next several hours. A part of her was angry that she hadn't stood up for herself and told them they were supposed to be going on a date. But more than anything she was just sad that Zach hadn't said anything either.

Right as she felt she was ready to rejoin them, her phone rang with a FaceTime call. She saw the name on the screen and froze.

Will <3

She stared at the photo of the tan face and curling copper hair that she had never quite forgotten even in the chaos of the first few months of school and living in New York City. Somehow it had slipped her mind to erase the heart next to his name, and they hadn't texted or called since the end of senior year last June, when they broke up amicably after several months of dating.

Before she could change her mind, Layla answered, and immediately Will's face appeared on her screen with his usual charming smile.

"Hello, Will," she said softly.

"I didn't think you would answer," Will said, almost embarrassed. "It's good to hear your voice."

"How are you doing?" Layla asked, unsure of what to say and not wanting to make it more awkward than it already was. "Is everything okay? Where are you? Are you still in Japan?"

Will had traveled with his moms to Japan, where one of his moms had family and also where they planned to relocate once they retired. He had backpacked for several weeks around the country and had been living somewhat off the grid. Layla remembered hearing from Vera that Will was thinking about moving there permanently to be closer to family.

"Actually, that's part of the reason I'm calling you," Will said with a smile. Then he lifted his camera up so that the white ceiling behind him bled into a large window overlooking a familiar skyline glittering in the night.

Layla's mouth fell open. "Is that—?"

"I'm in New York City!"

3

The following morning Aspen barely managed to get to work, her eyes swollen and her limbs heavy. Her colleagues kept asking her if she was okay, but she brushed them off by claiming to be tired after a long week. She probably looked like a living zombie. There were still no attempts of communication from Vera. Her heart crumbled because even though she knew their relationship was falling apart, she still clung to some form of delusional hope.

Aspen finished up her work day without a complaint, her body and mind reacting to her surroundings mechanically. Jenny came up to her when they were closing up.

"You look like you could use a drink," Jenny said, twisting a strand of hair on a ringed finger. "We're going to *The Apollo* if you want to join."

Aspen bit her lip. Usually she would say no, but what's the point now? Vera clearly didn't want her anymore, and besides, *she* was the one who told her to go party with her model friends. But that wasn't really why she said yes. Aspen said yes because finally there was a solution to her pain—getting completely wasted.

"I'm in," Aspen said finally.

"Well then follow me, babe," Jenny said, surprised that Aspen had actually agreed. As Aspen was following Jenny outside, she made a last-minute decision to text Vera.

Aspen: I'm going to the Apollo bar with some coworkers if you want to join.

She held her breath when she saw that Vera was typing, before disappointment welled up inside her as the typing dots disappeared. Either Vera was too busy to respond or she didn't care anymore to keep their relationship alive.

It didn't matter. She shoved her phone in her purse and followed Jenny into the car. There was no turning back now.

Aspen hasn't been this drunk since high school. She held onto Jenny's arm as they danced just to keep herself from tripping and falling on the ground.

The strobe lights blinded her and the music pounded through her eardrums. She could barely make out her own hands in the dark, and could only feel the dancing throngs of people pushing up against her.

Sweat dripped down her neck and her face was flushed. She whispered to Jenny that she needed water, then staggered to the bar, nearly missing the stool as she struggled to sit down.

The bartender came over to her. "For you, miss?"

Aspen ordered a margarita at the same time as a familiar voice spoke beside her. "And I'll have a Pale Ale."

She glanced to her right and the movement made her queasy. A tall, attractive guy with sandy brown hair and blue eyes leaned on the edge of the bar. It took Aspen a moment to recognize him. It was Jack, Sydney's ex-boyfriend, who was the girl Aspen had cheated with while she was still dating her boyfriend, Kyle.

"What are you doing here?" Aspen asked bluntly, the alcohol in her veins stripping her of all caution. Besides, they had never been friends, just unfortunate acquaintances.

Jack raised a brow. "I thought I would come say hello. It's been a while, and it's not every day in this city that you run into old classmates from Hilltop."

"Thought you'd hate me," Aspen muttered, grabbing the glass of her margarita when the bartender set it down in front of her. She took a sip and eyed Jack, trying to gauge his motive for approaching her.

"That was high school. And it wasn't your fault," Jack said, then grinned when Aspen raised a brow. "At least, it wasn't your fault that *my* girlfriend cheated."

Aspen leaned in, relishing in the way Jack's eyes involuntarily glanced down at her mouth. "Oh I wouldn't be too sure of that, *Jack*."

Jack's eyes darkened slightly, though in anger or attraction, Aspen couldn't tell. "Maybe you've had enough to drink."

He tried to call for the bartender and Aspen swatted his hand down. "I'm fine."

"Where's your girlfriend?" Jack asked, looking around. "I thought you were dating Layla's sister. What's her name? Vivian?"

"Vera," Aspen corrected sharply. "And she's not here."

"Oh?" Jack eyed her more carefully. "I think you should get home, don't you think?"

Aspen shook her head and took another long sip of her drink. He watched her wearily as she continued to drink until she drained the entire glass, just in case he had ideas about stealing it from her.

"Come on," she said after setting the empty glass down. "Dance with me."

Jack didn't say a word, only following her to the dance floor. Aspen's head swayed, but the new alcohol seemed to rush into her system and give her new energy. She looked around but couldn't see Jenny or any of her colleagues.

"What about you?" Aspen asked. "Are you dating anyone?"

"Not since Sydney. No one ever seemed to compare to her." After he said the words, Jack blushed. "I don't know why I told you that."

Aspen placed her hands on his hips, if only to see his reaction. "You really loved her, didn't you?"

Jack lowered his eyes, placing his hands on her hips hesitantly. They were not really dancing, but swaying to the beat in one place. "I did, yes."

"Can't you forgive her?" Aspen asked. "What if it was just a one-time mistake?"

His mouth tightened. "I can never forgive her."

She was just about to respond with a few choice words about *his* behavior in high school when she saw a familiar face across the dance floor, their eyes locking. Her hands dropped from Jack's waist, and Aspen craned her neck just in time to see Vera's red glasses and short hair disappear back into the crowds.

Aspen's face grew hot. "I-I need to go."

"Wait, Aspen—"

She didn't let him finish, running towards the exit

where Vera had rushed out after seeing Aspen dancing with a stranger. Did Vera think she was cheating on her? What was she doing, dancing with *Sydney's* Jack of all people?

Aspen swallowed bile that rose in her throat, pushing open the front doors and walking out to the street where she spotted Vera walking back to her car.

"Vera!" she called out. "Wait!"

Vera opened her driver's door and glared at her before getting in, and Aspen saw the tears glittering there before she slid inside and angrily drove off. She only realized the tears in her own eyes when she was struggling to catch her breath.

Footsteps. "Aspen, are you okay?"

It was Jack, standing behind her.

She tried to take a deep breath in but felt her stomach roll and heave.

"Aspen, who was that?"

"Oh no," she whispered.

Her stomach heaved again, and this time she barely had time to rush towards the edge of the street before she threw up. Strong hands held back her hair and spoke her name. The edges of her vision were tinted black as another wave of vomit rose up and past her throat.

"I'm sorry," she mumbled, her hands on her knees and

her chest rising and falling rapidly. "Fuck."

"It's okay," Jack said gently. "It's okay. Just breathe."

At last Aspen stood up, teetering on her heels. She felt embarrassed and thought she might have to throw up again soon. "I want to go home."

"I'll take you home," Jack said without hesitation.

"No."

"I have a car here and I only drank a beer."

Aspen hesitated. She felt that it was a bad idea to let him drive her home, but she also didn't want to pay for another ride after the dent she made in her bank account buying drinks. After all, he wasn't exactly a stranger. He was more like an ex, if only by association.

"I promise I'll leave once I make sure you're okay," Jack said quietly. His blue eyes were so sincere that Aspen knew she would relent. She could see why Sydney had fallen for him in the first place.

She pointed a finger at him. "Fine. But don't think this means anything."

His eyes widened in mock fear. "I wouldn't dare."

The car ride was silent at first as Aspen guided him towards her apartment. She glanced over at Jack, his strong arms while he gripped the steering wheel. He had played football in high school and was good enough to be accepted by UCLA to play for the team, even though she was sure he never got off the bench.

"How do you like the city?" Aspen asked, saying the first thing that came to mind.

Jack shrugged. "I like my teammates."

"But the city?"

"It's strange," Jack said slowly. "Not what I imagined it would be like. And you?"

Aspen sighed. "Same."

"Who was that girl you ran after? Was it Vera?"

"Yes," Aspen said, her stomach twisting uneasily as she imagined what Vera was thinking right now. "I invited her but I thought she wouldn't come. She never comes to these things. Then she did and she saw us together, so now I look like the bad guy when she was the one who stopped spending time with me in the first place."

"That sounds…complicated."

"But it's not, really," Aspen said, her eyes stinging with tears she refused to shed. "In the end, I love her a lot more than she loves me."

Jack shook his head. "That's not how it looked to me."

Aspen was silent.

When she didn't respond, Jack said, "If you really love

her, then you should fight for her."

She shot him a pointed look. "I could say the same for you."

They reached her apartment a few minutes later. Aspen got out of the car, Jack following close behind her. Together they walked up her steps in silence. Aspen wondered if Jack was going to kiss her and prepared herself to push him away.

"I'll leave you here," Jack said before she turned around, one step below her. "You can get inside without my help, right?"

Aspen rolled her eyes. "Yes, thank you."

Jack nodded. "Have a good night, Aspen."

"Wait." He paused on the next step. "Why did you really talk to me tonight? And don't say it's because I went to Hilltop. We both know we were never friends."

"I'm not sure," Jack said, then paused, looking out at the low skyline of trees and houses stretching for endless miles around them. "I guess because you looked lonely sitting at the bar and it reminded me of how I feel most nights." He half-smiled. "And I thought I could get revenge on Sydney."

"I have a girlfriend," Aspen said automatically, though she immediately felt that gnawing sadness after she spoke the words. "And I've changed a lot since high school."

Jack shook his head ruefully as he walked down the remaining steps to his car. "Good night, Aspen. And stay safe."

Aspen sighed. "Good night, Jack."

He merely nodded and got into his car. Aspen watched him drive away and disappear around the street corner before heading inside.

4

L ayla adjusted the hem of her shirt over her jeans and brushed down her fly-away hairs. In the reflection of the mirror, she saw Zach roll over in bed and look at her. It was already noon on a Saturday, but Zach wouldn't start getting out of bed until the early afternoon.

Last night she had silently endured dinner with Zach and his band, listening to one inside joke after another that she did not understand, and trying to ignore the way Zach and Gianna made eye contact. She knew they had once dated but Zach had made it very clear from the beginning of their relationship that he and Gianna were over. A part of her wondered if she was being naive, but then she reminded herself that she was about to get coffee with her ex. Two could play at this game

"Do I look good?" Layla asked, turning in place to show him her outfit.

Zach's brows furrowed. "Where are you going?"

"I'm meeting up with Will." Layla ignored his eyes and

grabbed her purse. "He's visiting New York City and asked to get coffee."

"Will…" Zach looked at her quizzically. "Who's that?"

Layla paused, wondering if she should lie and force him to pry the answer out of her, just like he had with Gianna. Instead, Layla decided to tell the truth, if only to see his reaction.

"You don't remember? He's my sister's friend from back home," Layla said, then glanced at him innocently. "I dated him for almost a year in high school. But it was nothing, don't worry."

Zach nodded, then cracked a grin. "I'm not worried, babe."

The comment irked her and she struggled to smile as she left his apartment. She had secretly hoped Zach would walk past and see her talking to Will, but clearly he wasn't jealous in the slightest.

Soon all thoughts of Zach melted away. Her heart began to beat faster as she walked down the street to the nearest bagel shop where Will had agreed to meet her.

"Layla."

She froze at the sound of his voice just before she reached the door. She looked up. Will stood across from her, his curls a dark copper in the late morning sun as they fell over his forehead, which was still tan from the summer. He had a brush of freckles across the bridge of his nose that Layla had always loved.

"Will," she whispered, then cleared her throat. "It's good to see you."

He didn't answer her but took a few steps and hugged her. His arms were a familiar embrace around her and she had the strange urge to cry. But then Will pulled away, and she tried to breathe normally again.

"Bagels?" she asked, to give her a moment to compose herself.

Will smiled, then opened the door for her. She walked inside, realizing that she was smiling too. They ordered their bagels and coffee and took a seat in the corner of the small shop. The only other people inside were an elderly man with his dog and a couple in workout clothes.

"So…how's Japan?" Layla asked, wanting to fill the awkward silence. She was so accustomed to Zach's quick conversation that she forgot Will was more reserved.

"I love it," Will said easily, glancing around the shop. "What about you? How is New York? And fashion school?"

Layla nodded. "I love it."

They both laughed nervously, and before the awkwardness could settle their names were called to get their bagels. Will handed over her bagel and coffee before grabbing his, then Layla suggested they walk to Tompkins Square Park.

"What else have you been up to?" Will asked. "Any fun plans for Thanksgiving?"

"Not much besides school and friends," Layla said, then cleared her throat. "I'm actually going to tour New England with my boyfriend's band during the break."

"Boyfriend?"

Layla glanced at him in surprise. "Vera didn't tell you?"

Will's cheeks colored the slightest red. "Well, no. I haven't spoken much to anyone while I've been in Japan. But that's great. I'm happy for you. What's his name?"

"Zach."

"And he's in a band?" Will asked doubtfully.

"Yeah," she said quietly. "It's pretty casual. Only been two months."

"I see." Will sipped his coffee.

"What about you? How is Japan?" Layla asked, quickly changing the subject.

Will smiled. "Japan is amazing. It's such a beautiful country and I've improved my Japanese a lot by being there these past few months. I've also gotten to spend time with family I don't see that often. My parents are thinking of moving there permanently once they retire."

"Are you planning to stay there too?" Layla asked.

"I'm not sure," Will said honestly. "I took a gap year after graduation to figure that out. But now I'm applying to colleges in the States, so I think for now I'll live in the US."

Layla bumped his shoulder playfully. "Ooh, are you applying to any in New York?"

Will laughed and nodded. "Yes, actually. That's part of the reason I came here. I'm touring NYU and Columbia."

"So you didn't come here just to see me?" Layla teased.

Instead of laughing, Will's eyes softened. "I did want to see you, Layla. I hope you don't take this the wrong way but…I've missed you over the summer."

Layla felt her throat tighten. "I've missed you too."

They briefly met eyes and Layla had to look away, her face hot. It felt wrong, as if she were betraying Zach in admitting it, but there was nothing wrong with missing…a friend of sorts. Besides, Zach looked at Gianna like that without remorse and they had dated for four years.

Once they reached the park, they sat down on a bench overlooking the browning lawns bordered by black fences. It was a nice day for early November, and most trees still held onto their orange and red leaves, though some had already piled up on the ground. Layla saw several couples strolling the grounds with their pets and groups of friends picnicking in cozy sweaters and puffy jackets.

For a moment, Layla imagined that Will was still her boyfriend and they were on a date together. She glanced at him, a smile in his eyes when he caught her looking at him biting into his bagel.

"What?" he asked after he swallowed, amusement in his eyes.

"Nothing." She looked at him a little longer, the smooth planes of his face so familiar that it hurt not to touch. "I was trying to remember why we broke up."

Will raised a brow. "Was it that forgettable?"

Layla couldn't help but laugh and lightly shove his arm as she used to when they bantered. "Come on, you know what I mean. I feel like we didn't have a real reason to break up like other couples do. We didn't even have a fight."

"We decided we wouldn't do long distance," Will said slowly. "I was going to Japan, you were going to New York…it seemed impossible back then."

"Back then?" she asked as a joke, though she knew they were walking a very dangerous line now. A part of her didn't care.

Will looked at her pointedly. "I'm not the one in a new relationship, Layla."

She frowned. "You haven't seen anyone since me?"

"No, I haven't." He balled up the paper bag his bagel had been wrapped in and stood up. "I should probably get going. The tour at Columbia starts in an hour."

"Right," Layla said, feeling flustered. She thought they had been joking but now it felt more like they had been arguing. "It was nice seeing you."

Will looked around the park, awkwardly scratching at his neck. He seemed to be debating something in his head before he spoke again. "I'll be around for the next few days. Would you want to hang out again?"

Layla felt her stomach twist with guilt. She thought of Zach at her apartment, oblivious to the thoughts in her head. But then she remembered how little he cared that she was reuniting with her ex. Suddenly she had an idea.

"What if you came to Zach's show tonight?" Layla asked. "His band is playing in Soho at some college party. It would be fun!"

He hesitated. "Are you sure Zach won't mind?"

Layla laughed, and she was surprised at how cold it sounded. "He won't mind at all."

The clock on Zach's bedside table ticked with an annoying clicking sound that was so loud Layla considered smashing it to pieces. It was already well past eight o'clock at night and Zach hadn't come home from band rehearsal. He probably decided to get dinner with his bandmates and couldn't make the time to stop by, even though he had promised he would see her before his show.

Layla had already gotten dressed in a short black mini skirt and cropped white-knit sweater that ran tightly across her shoulders, leaving her midriff bare but her arms warm. It was the kind of outfit Zach never complimented. Tonight it felt like revenge.

She just finished pouring herself a glass of vodka and cranberry juice when Aspen called her. Layla hastily picked up the phone, sensing bad news. "Aspen? Is everything okay?"

Aspen sighed on the other line. "I think I made a mistake. A big one."

Layla's stomach dropped. The last time Aspen had said those words she had cheated on her boyfriend at a party with a girl. "What did you do?"

"Well I didn't *do* anything," Aspen said irritably. "Except, Vera might think I did."

Dread washed over her at the sound of her sister's name. "What happened, Aspen?"

"Again, *nothing* happened. Last night I went out with

my coworkers and I got a little too drunk," Aspen said. "While I was at the bar, Jack came up to me and started talking—"

"Wait," Layla interrupted. "Jack? Who's Jack?"

Aspen paused, then answered quietly, "Sydney's Jack. From high school. He goes to UCLA now."

"*Sydney's* Jack?" Layla repeated, her voice raising involuntarily. "You spoke with *Sydney's* Jack?"

"*He* came up to *me*," Aspen said defensively. "It was so unexpected I didn't know what to say. We spoke a little but he said I was too drunk and thought I should go home. Of course, I said no. So I asked him to go to the dance floor and we danced together. But not *together* together, because he knew I had a girlfriend, and he was very respectful, and definitely still in love with Sydney—"

Layla sighed. "Okay, get to the point."

"Long story short, I forgot that I had invited Vera and she saw me dancing with Jack."

"Aspen, that's really bad! What happened next?"

"I ran after her but she got in her car and drove. Then I threw up a lot and Jack drove me back home. End of story."

Layla's head spun with the realization of what Vera must be thinking. "And you spoke with Vera, right? Explaining the situation?"

Aspen groaned. "I couldn't! We were already fighting, so this just made it worse. She's going to break up with me, Layla, I know it."

"Aspen, listen to me right now," Layla said slowly. "Go find her and apologize. Even if she breaks up with you, my sister deserves that much."

"But—"

"That was not a suggestion, Aspen." Layla glanced at the time and hopped off the bed. "Look, I have to get going. Zach is having a show tonight. Good luck with Vera. Promise me you'll talk to her as soon as you can."

"You know, ever since I started dating Vera you're never on *my* side anymore," Aspen complained, surely accompanied by a childish pout. "Just because she's your sister doesn't mean I'm in the wrong."

Layla laughed. "But you're also not in the right. Tell me when you guys make up."

Soon after they said their goodbyes and Layla hung up. She had a party to get to.

5

Aspen stood nervously outside the dorm building with a bouquet of pink roses in one hand. She patted the other on her jeans to keep her palm from sweating. It felt like she was going on a first date—or worse, the last date before breaking up.

Go find her and apologize. Even if she breaks up with you, my sister deserves that much.

Layla was right, as much as she didn't want to admit it. Instead of trying to fix the situation, Aspen had run off crying like a child having a tantrum. Her drunk escapade was merely a way to put off the inevitable conversation they had to have.

At last the door to the building opened and Vera stood in the doorway. She had agreed to see Aspen in order to hear out her apology and explanation. Aspen secretly suspected that Layla had a hand in opening up her sister's heart.

"Come in," Vera said quietly. Aspen followed her inside. Her roommate was gone, leaving only a messy bed strewn with clothes on her side of the room.

Once they were inside, Aspen held out the flowers. "I'm sorry. Please let me explain."

Vera took the flowers silently and nodded at her bed. They both took a seat, Vera placing the flowers by her side. Aspen saw that Vera's eyes were red, as though she had cried before Aspen had arrived.

"Just for the record," Aspen said without preamble, "I did not make any move on Jack and I never planned on doing anything with him."

"Then why were you two dancing together?" Vera asked, her eyes looking up sharply at Aspen, and she saw they were filled with distrust.

Aspen shook her head in frustration. "I was drunk, okay? He approached me as a friend, then he said I was too drunk and tried to take me home. *Not—*" Aspen quickly amended at Vera's wide eyes, "—because he wanted to try anything. He knew I was dating you. He even asked about you."

"Never stopped anyone before," Vera muttered.

"Come on," Aspen said quietly, placing a hand on Vera's thigh. "We were just dancing. I would never cheat on you. You believe me, right?"

Vera closed her eyes as though in pain. "I don't know.

Did he drive you home?"

"Yes, but—"

"See?" Vera stood up and began pacing the floor anxiously. "Why would you let him do that? Why do you always have to take things too far?"

"Well, maybe because I threw up on the side of the street and my girlfriend drove off before letting me explain, so it was either that or pay for a ride!" Aspen threw up her hands. "Will you always think the worst of me? Why can't you just believe for once in your life that I love you and only you?"

Vera stared at her, but she did not answer.

"Whatever," Aspen said, standing up. She didn't even feel sad. She just felt tired. "This is not about me getting drunk at a bar after we had a fight. And this is not about me talking with Jack or whoever and getting a ride home. This is about you and me. This is about saving our relationship. Do you even love me anymore?"

"Aspen…" Vera looked at her in disbelief, but Aspen started towards the door anyway. "No, don't go."

"Why not, Vera?" she asked, turning around and motioning between them. "What's going on here? Tell me why I should stay, because I'm not sure you even have a reason anymore."

"Because it hurts!" Vera cried out, her voice trembling.

"It hurts more to see you leave than to have you stay and argue with you." She took a deep breath in and out to compose herself. At last, she looked at Aspen, her green eyes steady. "Please stay, Aspen."

Aspen nodded her head slowly, then sat beside Vera on the bed once more, looking around the room when an awkward silence fell between them. "Where's your roommate?"

"Soccer game." Vera examined her roommate's side of the room. "It really sucks living with someone."

"Is that why you don't want to live with me?" Aspen joked, then catching Vera's alarmed face, added quickly, "Too soon, I know."

Vera shook her head. "No, it's not that. I would love to live with you. But I worry that if something bad happens, I'll be stranded."

"Something bad? Stranded?" Aspen repeated incredulously. "Like I'll throw you out on the street if we break up?"

"I don't know," Vera said miserably. "I just don't want to get hurt."

"Are you talking about moving in or…falling in love?" Aspen asked the question and then blushed. They had already said *I love you* to each other over a year ago now, but this argument felt like it was about something different. While the beginning of their relationship was light and fun, like the first days of summer, as their lives grew more weighty with responsibilities, their relationship suddenly appeared flimsy in the face of their future plans.

"I guess I'm scared of moving in and getting used to loving you only for you to discover two years down the line that you don't love me anymore." Vera bit her lip, eyes glancing up at the ceiling to keep her tears at bay. "And I know you could say you're scared of the same thing, but I *know* how I feel. I can't imagine myself not loving you for the rest of my life."

The words rushed through Aspen like a thrill, and she had to force herself to remain calm. "But that's how I feel too! I just don't know how I can prove it to you."

Vera shook her head, the tears spilling down her face at last, and when she spoke her voice trembled. "There are so many reasons for you not to be with me. One day you could meet a guy and realize you don't want to be with a girl your whole life. What if you don't want to deal with all the judgment? What if you want to have kids? A normal family?"

"Is that what you would tell Will and his two moms? That he doesn't have a normal family?" Aspen asked pointedly. "Besides, I could say the same thing to you.

What if you meet a girl who doesn't have a past mistake tainting your relationship with her? What if you get tired of dating a girl who isn't as smart as you?"

Vera looked at her in disbelief. "What? That doesn't matter to me."

"It seems like it does," Aspen said. "You never let me hang out with your engineering friends. I always think that you're embarrassed of me because I'm not as smart as them. Why else would you never introduce me?"

"Because *I'm* embarrassed of *them!*" Vera argued. "I always thought you would think they were nerdy or awkward. I didn't want you to meet them and decide I wasn't cool enough for you."

Aspen couldn't help but laugh. "Not cool enough? What is this, middle school?"

"You're the one who only hangs around hot models! Then you expect *me* to want to hang out with your friends just so I can see how many better options you have," Vera said, crossing her arms.

"First of all," Aspen said, taking Vera's arms and unraveling them, "they are my *coworkers,* not *friends.* You're basically my only friend." She pulled Vera closer. "Second of all, how could anyone compete with you when you're hot *and* smart?"

Vera tried to stop a reluctant smile. "You're such a flirt."

Aspen kissed her cheek, winding her arms around Vera's waist. "Is that a bad thing?"

"Oh it's bad," Vera murmured, finally giving in and bringing her hands up to Aspen's face and leaning in until their lips brushed. "Very, very bad."

Then they were kissing. Aspen couldn't help but smile against her mouth, sifting her fingers through Vera's hair. Her lips were so soft beneath hers, and her lip balm tasted like sugar. Without a word, Aspen dragged them back on the bed, pulling Vera on top of her.

"I'm still mad at you," Vera said crossly, looking down at Aspen with her shirt halfway up her stomach.

Aspen brushed her fingertips against the tender skin above Vera's waistline. "I can live with that for now."

Vera's eyes fluttered shut. "Aspen, my roommate…"

"—is not here yet." Aspen pulled Vera by the front of her shirt until they were kissing again. She felt hot all over, as though she were doused in fire. Vera's hands slid expertly up her shirt, tracing the lacy edge of her bra.

"We should stop," Vera whispered, slightly out of breath, but she only kissed Aspen again, her fingers already unhooking her bra.

Just as Aspen began lifting Vera's shirt, a violent ringing sound startled them apart. Vera groaned and rifled with the sheets until she found her phone. Her eyes widened when she saw the screen, then she glanced at Aspen in alarm.

"It's Layla," she said, then groaned again. "I have to answer it. I told her I would call after I talked with you."

Aspen raised a brow but did not protest.

"Hello?" Vera asked hesitantly, putting Layla on speakerphone.

"I'm surprised you answered," Layla said. Aspen smirked and continued inching her hands under Vera's shirt.

Vera glared at her. "Why?"

"Oh, I just thought you might be with Aspen."

Aspen's hands moved up and Vera stifled a noise. "Hmm."

Layla was silent for a moment, then, "She's there right now, isn't she?"

"Hi Layla," Aspen said sweetly, then laughed.

"I take it you guys made up already?" Layla asked dryly.

"Stop it," Vera hissed when Aspen tried to kiss her neck, craning her head away, though she couldn't hold back a smile. "Why did you call?"

Layla sighed. "It's probably a good thing you're both listening." She paused a beat. "Will is here. In New York."

"*My* Will?" Vera asked at the same time that Aspen said,

"You're kidding."

"Yeah, he's visiting to tour colleges," Layla explained. "But I think I made a mistake. We went to coffee and then I was scared I wouldn't see him again and I sort of wanted to make Zach jealous so I invited him to Zach's show tonight. I'm actually standing outside the venue right now. What do I do?"

"Is there something to be done?" Vera asked slowly, sharing a look with Aspen.

Layla laughed bitterly. "I guess not."

"Do you *want* to…do…something?" Aspen asked hesitantly. "What about Zach?"

There was no reply. They could hear wind rustling on the other line, and faint music and shouts in the distance. Vera took Aspen's hand in hers, frowning as the silence lengthened.

"Whatever you do," Vera said quietly, "follow your heart."

She lifted Aspen's hand and kissed her knuckles softly. Aspen felt her heart swell with a love as deep as the deepest ocean, yet more light than air. It seemed impossible, yet she hardly knew how she could live without it.

Suddenly Layla sucked in a breath. "I need to go. He's here."

Then she hung up, leaving Aspen and Vera in a

thoughtful silence.

6

Will strode towards her with an awkward wave as Layla hung up on Vera and Aspen. He was bundled up in a dark blue sweater and light wool coat over fitted jeans, as though he were going to a nice restaurant instead of a party.

"Hey," Layla said, her voice drowned out by the music blasting from the basement. "I'm glad you came."

"Me too." Will glanced at the door nervously. Layla noticed that he didn't step forward to hug her. "Have they started?"

"They just played the first song."

Will hesitated. "And your boyfriend really doesn't mind that I'm here?"

Layla had still not mentioned anything to Zach, but she only smiled. "Nope. Besides, he doesn't control who I can see or not."

"Of course." Then Will smiled to ease the awkwardness. "Let's go inside then."

Together they walked down the rickety metal staircase into the basement where crowds of college students and loyal fans had already gathered around a wooden stage. Two large speakers flanked the stage and the beat of the bass vibrated the floor with the sheer volume of sound.

Even from across the room, Layla could see Zach standing to the right of Gianna, a grin on his face as he played the guitar. He leaned teasingly towards some girls in the front row who screamed and craned their necks to take photos with him.

Will glanced at her with a raised brow but said nothing. She led him to the middle of the floor where there was a space in between the crowds. They stood next to each other stiffly. Layla tried to dance to the beat but failed, and saw out of the corner of her eye that Will was looking at her.

"What?" Layla asked.

"Nothing," Will said, shaking his head with a smile. He leaned in closer so that she would hear him over the music. "It's just that I never would have thought we would be here like this."

Layla laughed. "Like what? Friends?"

"I don't know…dancing at a college party in New York City," Will said, then added, "And also friends."

"Why wouldn't we still be friends?" Layla asked playfully, but her heart pounded in her chest, signaling that she was walking that thin line again.

Will looked at her steadily beneath his blonde lashes. "Because we never really *were* friends."

Layla tried to ignore the burning heat on her face and kept her voice light. "Then maybe we should try to be friends. You're still friends with my sister, aren't you?"

"That's different and you know it," Will said wryly. "Plus, Vera and I never kissed."

This time Layla had to look away from his blue eyes before she lost her breath entirely. She had always felt like that looking at him, as if he were too beautiful to be real, let alone standing in front of her. Even in high school, whenever she had seen Will, either hanging out with Vera or at school, Layla's breath would leave her, as though she had stumbled upon a beautiful ocean view where she least expected it.

She still remembered with intense clarity the first time they had kissed. Will had been at her house looking for Vera, but she wasn't at home. Instead of letting him leave, Layla had insisted that he stay for a little, though she never understood what possessed her to do so. While it wasn't the first time they had hung out together, they had never been alone before.

At the time, she was also casually seeing Julian, who she

knew only wanted to date her to sleep with her. Then suddenly there was Will, talking with her more than Julian had ever spoken with her, so kind and attentive, asking questions about her and laughing at her jokes. Still, it had come as a surprise when, as they hugged goodbye at the door, their eyes wandered down and Layla found herself kissing him. She had apologized at the same time as he had, Will muttering something about Vera and Layla stuttering about Julian. It had all happened so fast, and Will left hurriedly before they could talk about it.

But when Aspen and Vera started dating, Layla began seeing Will more often. They were never friends, even as they spent more time alone together, often flirting with each other and tiptoeing around their kiss. Then during the summer on a random Tuesday, Will asked her on a date.

Layla spent her senior year in an unreal haze. She could not believe that Will—smart, kind, beautiful Will—would even bother talking to her, let alone date her. That year was filled with double dates, impromptu road trips, and high school house parties where she and Will would try to sneak off to the backyard or a guest bedroom without their friends noticing. Despite what she had always heard about teenage boys, though, Will never pushed her to have sex and allowed her to initiate everything, so they took their time exploring slowly. It was a dream she never wanted to end.

Then summer rolled around and Will left for Japan. They had not slept together yet, and Layla was secretly terrified that Will resented her for it. She feared that he would want to break up with her now that they were graduating and he could find someone new and more ready than her. So in a brief conversation a week before his flight, she had blurted out that they should just remain friends and not try to date long-distance.

Will had respectfully agreed and that was that. No fighting, no pleading, just a quiet goodbye and a last glance from Will that was the only sign of his disappointment. A few months later, she had packed her bags and moved to New York, where she met Zach and barreled head-first into a new relationship. He was her first time, and though he was gentle and experienced, she had not felt the triumph and satisfaction she had expected after losing her virginity. And now, standing next to Will, whom she had always secretly thought would be her first, Layla had never felt more empty and regretful.

"I'm sorry I brought it up," Will said, noticing her silence. "I'm glad we can be friends."

Layla tried to smile but found that she couldn't joke about something so serious. "You know, I never said this before, but thank you for always treating me so well when we were together. I've never had a boy treat me like that."

"Zach doesn't treat you well?" Will asked in slight alarm.

"No," Layla said quickly. "He does. He just…doesn't treat me like you did. I don't think anyone ever will."

"Don't say that," Will said, placing a hand on her shoulder. "You deserve someone who loves you…who loves you as much as I did." His eyes lowered as he added in a half-murmur, "Any boy would be stupid not to."

She almost told him that Zach hadn't said *I love you* to her yet, but bit back the words. Her own heart could not bear to hear the words aloud. Instead, she smiled and took his hand.

"Thank you, Will," she said, then tugged at him. "Come on, let's dance!"

Amid the crowd they danced to the music, Gianna's voice hardly heard over the guitar and drums. Layla was secretly glad because she hated their lyrics and Gianna's voice annoyed her. After a few songs were played, Layla began to feel the effects of her at-home cocktail wear off.

"Do you wanna get a drink?" Layla asked, having to practically shout as they had migrated closer to a speaker. "I know where we can find some."

Will nodded and followed her as she wove through the crowd. She led them to a hallway that connected the stage with a side room and kitchen that was used by the band. Zach had played at this venue before and had shown her the way around.

"The band usually keeps alcohol in here for invited guests of the band," Layla said sweetly, opening the fridge. Sure enough, there were two cases of beer and seltzers inside, partially hidden by a left-over pizza box. "And since *I'm* an invited guest of a band member and *you're* my guest, we are entitled to at least one drink each." She grabbed two seltzers and gave one to Will, their cans cracking open with a fizz. "Cheers!"

"What are we cheering to in here?"

Layla froze at the voice. Zach stood in the doorway, looking at each of them with a smile, though she would not have called it kind. "Zach. What are you doing back here?"

Zach sauntered over to them. "Intermission. Thought I'd grab a can." He reached behind Layla and pulled out a can of beer. Then he clinked Will's seltzer. "Cheers, man. You must be Will."

"I am," Will said cautiously, then lifted his can slightly. "Thanks for the drink."

"Thanks for stopping by." Zach grinned before he took

a long gulp of his beer. His hair fell in damp strands over his forehead from the effort of performing. Layla used to think he looked sexy after playing all night, but next to Will, she thought his cutoff shirt looked cheesy and his hair unwashed. "How do you like the city?"

Will smiled briefly. "It's definitely one of a kind."

Zach slung a sweaty arm around Layla's shoulder, and she fought the urge to shrug him off. "Just like this girl right here." Then he leaned down and kissed her.

She stood without moving, her face heating up in embarrassment. Zach was clearly jealous now, and was trying to mark his territory. He kissed her one last time on the cheek before walking away.

"See you after the show, babe," Zach said with a wink as he backed into the hall.

Then he was gone. Layla could finally breathe. Will stared at the ground, a small frown on his face.

"I'm sorry," Layla said quietly.

This time Will looked embarrassed. "Don't be. He's your boyfriend." *Not me,* were the unspoken words, but his hardened eyes as he looked up at her spoke them anyway.

"We should go back to the show." Layla forced a smile. "I want to dance, and you're going to dance with me."

She squeezed them back through the crowds and into

the middle of the dance floor. While they were away the crowd had increased in size, so that everyone was pushing up against each other as they fought to be closer to the stage.

When the chorus of their most popular song came on, Layla lifted her arms and sang out loud with the rest of the crowd until Will smiled, his head bobbing to the beat. Her heart clenched painfully as she forced herself to stay put, to ignore his hands that hung at his sides, and his lips that curved in a smile.

Suddenly a body shoved into her and she pitched forward. She was narrowly saved from the cement ground by hands on her arms. She looked up. Will was so close, his eyes wide in concern. Layla couldn't stop herself from glancing down at his mouth. In that moment she knew she would trade ever kissing Zach again for one kiss with Will right now.

"Layla," Will said, his voice low. Almost a warning, but perhaps not only for herself.

She straightened herself up. "Thank you." Her voice wavered. "I think...I think I might—"

"No." Will's hand was still on her arm, and his grip had tightened, though he didn't look her in the eye. "I should go. I have an early tour tomorrow at NYU."

"Okay." She stepped away. Will's hand fell from her

arm. "Will I see you again?"

He hesitated, then nodded, his cheeks still tinged with a blush. "If you're free, just let me know."

A moment later and he was gone, disappearing through the crowds. Layla stood there without moving until someone accidentally shoved her again. Then she reluctantly made her way to the back room to wait for Zach and the night to end.

7

"Stop bouncing your leg, you're making me nervous," Vera whispered, glancing around the library.

"Why are you nervous?" Aspen shot back. "These are *your* friends. I'm the one who should be nervous."

Vera rolled her eyes. "They are harmless."

They returned to an anxious silence. Aspen looked around the library where they had planned to meet her friends after breakfast. It was the first time she had stepped foot inside, despite the many hours Vera had spent in here. Aspen always hated libraries, the deep silence grating on her nerves. She liked places where she could be loud and no one would look at her twice.

"There they are," Vera said, standing up and waving.

Across the room strode in a small group of normal-looking college kids with large backpacks on their shoulders. They came forward and waved at them awkwardly before taking seats around the table Vera had secured half an hour ago.

"Hi," Vera said once they were all settled, then gestured to Aspen. "This is my girlfriend, Aspen."

"Nice to meet you guys," Aspen said, looking around with a smile.

They all blinked at her. Most of them had glasses and were dressed in sweats and college sweatshirts. And they all looked exhausted. One of the girls with the friendliest smile and dark curly hair held out her hand.

"It's nice to meet you, Aspen," she said shyly. "My name is May."

"It's nice to meet you, May," Aspen said, trying to memorize the name with the face.

"And this is Julia, David, Omar, and Erin," May said, pointing to each one. They all smiled politely at Aspen, though she could tell they were very shy and reluctant to speak with a near stranger. May looked at Aspen. "So what school do you go to?"

Immediately Aspen's face heated up, and Vera stiffened beside her. "Oh, I'm not in school. I work at a modeling agency."

May's eyes widened. "You're a model?"

"Well, no, not yet," Aspen said, her stomach twisting nervously. "I'm just an assistant at a modeling agency."

"So you never went to college?" Julia—the only girl

without glasses—asked, her brows furrowed. She didn't seem to be insulting her, but Aspen felt the embarrassment cripple her inside anyway.

"Nope." Aspen tried to smile and failed as they all looked at her in slight bewilderment. "I was never a very good student. College just wasn't worth it for me, and you don't need a degree to be a model."

"Right, okay. That's cool!" Julia offered her a smile, then turned to Vera excitedly. "Did you see what Professor Gamble sent us? The exam is pushed to next Thursday."

"Oh thank god," Vera said, her eyes brightening.

Then they began chatting about one of their classes and how they planned to study for the exam. Aspen sat silently as they spoke about things she did not know. Their conversation turned to their latest engineering homework and they discussed specific lessons with terminology that Aspen had never heard before.

Vera hardly looked at her. Once the others were speaking about their studies their faces became animated and they spoke without hesitation, their initial shyness at seeing Aspen dissipating with each minute. After an hour, Aspen wasn't sure they even remembered she was there.

To hide her discomfort, Aspen went on her phone and scrolled through social media, although this eventually made her feel even more stupid as the others pulled out their homework and debated the answers to very complicated-sounding questions.

Aspen placed a hand on Vera's arm, who jumped slightly at the contact, as if she had forgotten she was still there. "I think I should go."

"Now?" Vera asked in surprise.

"I don't have anything to study," Aspen said, gesturing to the notebooks and textbooks now piled up on the desk. The others studiously avoided looking at them, pretending to read something or rifle through their backpacks. "I'm gonna go."

Vera bit her lip, conflicted, then nodded. She stood up. "I'll walk you out."

Aspen felt that familiar shame settle inside her, as though she were a burden, and somehow embarrassing Vera just by being next to her.

"You didn't have to walk me out," Aspen muttered as they approached the door.

Once they were outside, Vera turned on her. "Why are you acting like this? I thought this was what you wanted."

"I wanted *you* to want me there," Aspen said, looking at the ground and blinking away tears. She didn't want to cry, but her eyes already burned.

Vera threw her hands up. "I don't get you, Aspen! I'm

trying."

"You barely spoke with me for a second once your friends arrived!" Aspen exclaimed, ignoring a few strange looks from students entering the library. "I was like a piece of furniture. You guys talked about engineering the whole time and made me feel stupid, just like I knew would happen. Now they think I'm a loser for not going to college."

"Well it's not *my* fault *you* chose not to go to college," Vera shot back, crossing her arms.

Aspen had the urge to laugh. "What is that supposed to mean?"

"You chose not to go to college and continue your education. You chose to try and be a model knowing the chances were slim. Now you blame it on my friends?"

"Is this a joke?" Aspen laughed aloud, but it was cold. "All this time I thought you were supporting my dreams but really you were talking about how dumb I am with your smart engineering friends behind my back?"

"Actually, I never told them you weren't in college," Vera said pointedly.

"That was obvious." Aspen crossed her arms. "So you think—what? I should quit my job and go back to school?"

Vera leveled her with a serious look. "Aspen, I don't

want you to give up on your dream. But at some point, you have to think practically about this. Will modeling really secure you a future?"

"You make a perfect engineer," Aspen said viciously. "Everything is always practical with you."

"Well, it's the real world, Aspen! Are you just going to be an assistant for the rest of your life?"

"Maybe I will be! So what? Is this what's been truly bothering you about me? God, Vera, I thought you supported me."

"I do support you!" Vera sighed, rubbing her face. "I do, Aspen, but I also worry about you. And your future. That's all. Especially…especially if that future includes me."

Aspen was silent.

"I'm sorry I made you feel ignored in there," Vera continued quietly. "My friends are nice, but I admit they lack some social etiquette sometimes. Product of the engineering major, unfortunately. But I should have tried harder to keep you in the conversation."

"It's okay," Aspen relented. "I'm sorry I left like that."

Vera half-smiled. "It was getting boring. Even I need a break from it sometimes."

"Speaking of breaks, you should come to this party tonight," Aspen said, taking Vera's hand in hers. "My coworker—Jenny, you've met her before—is celebrating her birthday at *The Apollo* at eight. I can pick you up on the way and we'll go together."

"*The Apollo* again?"

Aspen rolled her eyes. "It's Jenny's favorite bar. Can you come or not?"

"I don't think I can," Vera said, her cheeks tinged red. "It's a Sunday night."

"But you don't have class on Mondays," Aspen argued. "Come on, it'll be fun. I just met your friends, so you should hang out with mine."

"My friends are nice."

Aspen raised a brow. "They barely spoke to me. My coworkers are nice too. Half of them are gay. It'll be so fun!"

"I don't know..." Vera's face held a hesitation that seemed different from the ones she was voicing.

"Why not?"

Vera dropped Aspen's hand, and a coldness that left her untouchable cloaked Vera's face. "I don't know. I just don't want to go."

Aspen tried to take a deep breath but she could only feel that buzzing panic, as though Vera had already broken up with her. She didn't understand Vera's resistance. Did she really love her? Was she scared of more commitment? Or was this all secretly about Aspen's flaws, her past mistakes and her uncertain future?

"I should get back inside," Vera added, glancing at the library doors.

"If that's what you want."

Vera opened her mouth as if she were going to say something, then closed it. She gestured to the library. "They're waiting for me."

Aspen watched her go back inside as her dread curled into anger. Vera hadn't even kissed or hugged her good-bye. Was she even going to see her again? It was as though every time Aspen tugged her closer, Vera found another way to unravel them farther apart.

Once she was back in her apartment, Aspen called Layla, hoping that she had an idea of what was going on in Vera's head.

"Oh thank god you called," Layla said hurriedly. "I need to talk with you about Will."

Aspen pushed down a wave of annoyance. "What about him? Is he still in New York?"

"I'm going to get dinner with him today. Then we're going to walk along the river."

"That sounds romantic," Aspen deadpanned.

Layla was silent for a moment. Then, "I know. Zach saw him at the show. It was really awkward. He kissed me in front of Will and everything."

"Ouch."

"Do you even care?" Layla snapped, catching on to Aspen's tone.

"I'm sorry," Aspen said with a sigh. "I just have a lot going on with Vera."

"What? I thought you two made up."

"We did, sort of. Then I met her engineering friends and they ignored me and we had a fight about it." Aspen lay back on the bed, the energy sapped from her limbs. She dreaded the birthday party she would have to go to alone. "I just don't know what to do. I'm so scared of losing her."

"Did you ever think that Vera's scared of losing you too?" Layla asked.

"That's not what it looks like," Aspen said dryly. "She never hangs out with me or wants to go out with me. She doesn't want me to meet her friends. She acts like she's busy twenty-four-seven and doesn't make the time for me. I'm the one who's actually *trying* here!"

Layla hesitated. "I think you're missing the point."

"Is there something you know that I don't?" Aspen asked, hearing that telltale sign of a secret in Layla's voice.

"There are some things that have to stay between sisters," Layla said reluctantly. "But I know that she loves you. She's just…scared."

"I am too, Layla," Aspen said, staring up at the ceiling. She knew Layla would tell her nothing more about Vera. That was the consequence of dating your best friend's sister. "So what are you going to do about Zach?"

"What about him?"

"Layla," Aspen said, "you don't even like him. I know you. When you were with Will, you couldn't stop talking about him. You were so in love."

"Yeah, well that love is gone."

"Is it?"

"Aspen! You're not helping."

"Just don't make the same mistake as me," Aspen warned jokingly. "Break up with Zach before you kiss Will."

"I'm not going to kiss Will!" Layla exclaimed, sounding scandalized.

Aspen laughed. "Oh, Layla. I guess we're *both* missing the point."

8

Layla stared up at the ceiling. It must've been nearing late afternoon, though she hadn't bothered to check the time. Zach was gone rehearsing with his band for another show tonight that she would not be attending.

He had gotten drunk by the time they left the party last night, which was in the early hours of the morning. He had stumbled inside the apartment, turned, and grabbed Layla, kissing her roughly. Then he had moved her to the bed and taken off her clothes with a passion that Will had never shown.

Only a week ago she would've thought it all romantic, but now she just felt cheap. He had passed out shortly afterward and lay snoring softly beside her. But Layla couldn't sleep. She kept thinking of Will, his soft blue eyes, the pressure of his hand on her arm. *You deserve someone who loves you…who loves you as much as I did.*

Did that mean he didn't love her anymore? Layla didn't know why that bothered her, since she had apparently moved on much quicker than he had. But still, the thought that Will's love for her had faded made her feel slightly nauseous. *You were so in love.*

Aspen was right. Layla had been in love. So, so in love. Will had been her Prince Charming, a dream come true that had to end when the clock struck midnight. She had thought it was a fantasy, something that was too good to be hers, and when it ended and she got to college, she settled on the first boy who gave her attention, kissing him until she thought Will's memory had been burned from her mind.

But Aspen was wrong in one thing. She wasn't going to kiss Will. Clearly he wasn't in love with her anymore, and besides, she had a boyfriend. And she liked Zach. Or did. She didn't know what she wanted now. Did she long for Will? Or the girl she used to be before she met Zach?

Her phone buzzed on the nightstand. She had taken a nap and only just woken up. She reluctantly picked up her phone.

Will: *I'll be there in ten.*

Layla's heart stopped and she scrambled out of bed. She had forgotten what time she had agreed to see Will for dinner. He was leaving in a few days back to Japan, so she figured this might be the last time she got to see him for a while. If she was also secretly trying to make Zach jealous, it was not at the forefront of her mind as she rushed to put on jeans and a cute t-shirt under her coat. It was the kind of simple outfit she used to wear back home, and suddenly she felt seventeen again, kissing Will on the porch of her house.

Once she was dressed, she made her way downstairs to the lobby of the apartment. Will was already outside, huddled in his puffer. He saw her and his eyes brightened as he smiled at her.

"Hey," Layla said, stepping out into the chilly evening air.

"Hey," Will replied, still smiling. "Where are we going?"

She tried not to look into his eyes, as if that could shield her from her own heart. "It's a Puerto Rican restaurant nearby that I like. Then I thought we could go walk by the river."

"Sounds romantic," Will joked, just like Aspen had, then he saw her face and his smile dropped. "Sorry," he added quickly. "Bad joke. Which way is the restaurant?"

Layla raised a brow at his choice of humor but didn't comment. "This way."

They walked together towards the restaurant, exchanging harmless pleasantries. Will talked about his tours and the sights he had seen around New York, while

Layla made fun of him for falling into all the obvious tourist traps.

A few blocks later they reached the restaurant and were led to a table that Layla had reserved earlier for them. She glanced at Will as they sat down at the table for two and blushed when he was looking right back at her.

"So…" Will began with an awkward smile once they had ordered their food, "do you know what you want to do after college?"

"It's a little too early for that, don't you think?" Layla asked, taking a sip of her water.

Will shrugged. "You always seemed like the kind of girl who knew what she wanted."

Layla bit back the words *I was*. "I knew I wanted to go into fashion. When I was dressed nicely, I felt more confident, so I wanted to share that confidence with the world. But now…I don't know. There's a million girls like me in New York."

Will's brows furrowed. "Layla, you're—"

"—one of a kind?" Layla finished teasingly. "I know. It's not that." She sighed. "I guess my dream is just starting to look more like reality. New York is everything I wanted, but I also miss my old life. My childhood friends who loved me for me and not for what clothes I wore or what parties I went to, my family being nearby, the peace and quiet of my block, going to the beach every weekend." Layla gestured towards the windows where the sky had already darkened to a night black. "The sun."

Will nodded thoughtfully. "You miss what you know the best. That's normal. But sometimes we have to get out and see the world to know what we love most in it."

Layla was silent. *You were so in love.*

"I used to think that I would travel around Japan and come back knowing who I was and what I wanted in my life," Will continued quietly.

"Did you?"

Will half-smiled. "No. If anything, I think I realized that being young is not knowing what you want in life. It's part of the fun."

"It doesn't feel like fun," Layla said wryly. "It feels like walking along the edge of a cliff blindfolded."

"But that's what friends are for." Will glanced at her hand that was resting on the table. "We hold hands and walk together."

Layla's face was warm, and she hid her blush with a smile. She wished they could order drinks, but she wouldn't be of age for another two years. The rest of dinner passed uneventfully, with Will describing his travels in Japan and Layla explaining her coursework and final projects.

Once they paid for dinner—Will insisted on paying and after much protest Layla accepted—they walked out of the restaurant and Layla silently steered them in the opposite direction of the apartment.

Their conversation petered out as they walked under the streetlamps and glittering skyscrapers, and Layla couldn't help but think how romantic this felt. At last they reached the glittering water of the East River. Layla led them south so that they could see the Williamsburg Bridge lit up in the distance.

Layla's heart pounded painfully in her chest as they slowed to a stop at the railing overlooking the water. Will stood beside her, gazing out at the shoreline across the river, his curls trembling in the breeze. If this were truly a date, now was the time they would kiss. The thought sent a thrill through her, then a sudden dread at what she might do.

She turned to him. "Will, I—"

"Don't," Will said, his voice rough. He turned towards her reluctantly, his face rigid, as though it took every muscle in his body to force himself to look at her. His eyes were longing when he did. "Don't say anything."

Layla stared at him, the words lodged in her throat, even though she wasn't sure what they were going to be. I miss you? I still love you? I wish I could take it all back and still be with you? It was impossible. She had a boyfriend now. Will was returning to Japan. Yet as she looked into his soft blue eyes, his lips parted, standing only a few inches apart, only one thought crossed her mind.

"I really want to kiss you," Will whispered, so low Layla doubted she heard correctly.

His gaze dropped, though his hands remained balled in fists at his side and he stood ramrod straight. Layla nearly leaned in, the weight of her body dragged forward as it had been the very first time.

Then she turned abruptly, stepping away, her breath shallow. "This was a bad idea."

Will stepped away too, a grim smile on his face as he grabbed the railing with both hands. "I'm sorry. I shouldn't have said that."

"No, it's…" Layla sighed. "It's my fault."

"No," Will said coldly. "I wasn't thinking. It's just been a long time since I've been in a romantic setting like this with someone…someone I used to love. It brought back old feelings that don't mean anything now. That's all."

The words stung her even though she knew Will was trying to preserve her innocence in the act they had almost committed. "Don't worry," Layla said, her voice equally cold. "It doesn't mean anything to me either."

"Are you going to tell Zach?" Will asked bitterly.

Layla crossed her arms. "No. Nothing happened, right?"

"Right."

His preoccupation with Zach annoyed her. "Why would you care if I told him or not anyways? It's not like you're *best friends* with him or something. You did that one already, haven't you?"

Will masked a flash of hurt with a tight smile. "Weren't you the one who kissed your *sister's* best friend and then got angry when she did the same to you? Or did you already forget about that?"

"Sometimes I wish I could," Layla shot back with an equally tight smile. They were fighting now, as if the fight they should've had when they broke up was coming out all these months later.

"Same." Will turned away angrily. "I thought we could still be friends, but clearly we can't. I should never have come here."

"I thought you came to visit colleges?"

He glared at her. "Of course I did."

"Oh, so you didn't come here to see if I was still single?" Layla demanded. "Because that's sure what it looked like a minute ago when you tried to kiss me."

"That was a mistake," Will said sharply.

"And so was this."

Before he could respond, Layla turned and stalked off. She left him standing there, exactly as she had been left that day before summer, except this time she let herself cry.

9

Aspen checked the clock on her bedside table, then looked at her outfit in the mirror, adjusting the tight black leather skirt a little lower on her thighs. She sighed. There was no reason for her to delay any longer, and soon Jenny would be asking where she was.

Her phone rang as she shoved her lipstick and keys into her purse. It was Layla. Despite this being the second time they were calling today, Aspen was grateful for any excuse to linger at her apartment.

"Hello?"

"Aspen?" Layla asked meekly, sniffling.

"Are you crying?" Aspen demanded. "What happened? Did Zach do something to you?"

"No." She paused. "It was Will."

Aspen gasped. "Oh god, did you kiss him?"

"No! But he tried to," Layla said, taking a shaky breath in. "And I almost did. But then he acted like it meant nothing afterward."

"He was just saying that." Aspen shook her head. "He's clearly still in love with you if he flew all the way to New York to see you."

Layla laughed bitterly. "Only because he was visiting colleges here."

"Riiiight. And you believe that?"

"I don't know," Layla said, her voice trembling. "I don't know what I believe anymore."

"You should talk with Zach," Aspen said. "He's your boyfriend. Maybe if you tell him how you're feeling about things then you'll get more clarity."

"I doubt that," she muttered. "But I should probably talk to him anyway."

Aspen grabbed her jacket by the door. "I wish I could talk more, Layla, but I have to go."

"Where are you going? Are you meeting Vera?"

"Nope," Aspen said, opening the door and walking outside. "I'm going back to *The Apollo* for my coworker Jenny's birthday party. Vera didn't want to come."

"Jenny?"

"Yes. Why?"

"Nothing," Layla said quickly. "Well, have fun!"

Aspen said goodbye and walked out to the curb, where her ride was already waiting. She thought idly about taking a ride to UCLA instead and seeing if Vera would change her mind but then thought better of it. If Vera wanted to come, she could drive there herself.

Fifteen minutes later she arrived at *The Apollo,* which hadn't begun to get crowded yet. She walked inside and was immediately greeted by the cheers of her coworkers who gathered around her excitedly. Jenny approached her and gave her a hug. She wore a tight velvet red dress, her blonde hair straight as a pin and cut right above her shoulders.

"You look so hot!" Aspen exclaimed to the agreement of the others. "You could star in a James Bond movie in that dress."

Jenny pretended to shoot a gun at Aspen's chest and then blew the smoke from her fingertip. "Then you better watch out. You might just be my next target."

Aspen laughed. "I'd like to see you try."

"Come on," Jenny said, looping her arm in Aspen's. "Let's get a drink."

They walked together to the bar, where they ordered their drinks. Jenny left her tab open, but Aspen asked to close hers.

At this Jenny gave her a strange look. "Not drinking more?"

Aspen shook her head. "I got too drunk last time. I'm gonna be more careful tonight."

"Ah, I see," Jenny said slowly, then smirked. "Would you do one shot with me though? For my birthday? Please?"

"Fine. But make it tequila please, not vodka."

Jenny laughed and ordered the two shots, which they downed before biting into their limes. Then Jenny dragged Aspen to the dance floor, which had already started to fill up as the night wore on. Their other coworkers found them and together they all danced and sang along to a mix of 80's pop songs which this bar liked to play.

After an hour, Aspen noticed that she and Jenny had migrated away from the rest of their party and found themselves in a quiet corner of the dance floor.

"Having fun?" Jenny asked, nudging her shoulder. Aspen had been quiet for some time.

"Yes," Aspen said, forcing a smile, though she hadn't stopped thinking about Vera all alone in her dorm room. The drink and shot were enough to make her consider calling her. "Thank you for inviting me."

Jenny smiled brilliantly. "Of course! You're one of my closest friends."

"Really?" Aspen had never thought of Jenny like that before.

"I mean, I think you're really cool," Jenny said with a

stunning, red-lipped smile. "And beautiful."

"Thank you, Jenny," Aspen said in surprise. Jenny had never complimented her so openly before. "You are too."

Then Jenny placed a hand on her arm and leaned in with a seductive glint in her eyes. "Would you ever want to get drinks sometime? Just us?"

Shock and then dread washed over Aspen as she realized what this had all been about. God, she was so stupid sometimes. "I'm sorry Jenny. I have a girlfriend." Her face was hot in embarrassment, though for Jenny or herself she didn't know. "I thought you knew," she added awkwardly.

Jenny leaned back, her face paling. "Oh shit. I'm so sorry. I just—I thought you guys broke up or something, I mean, I haven't seen her with you since that one time…"

"Well, we're still together," Aspen said tightly. "I'm sorry if I gave you the wrong impression."

"I see. Then I guess I should get back to the others," Jenny said, stiffly motioning to the rest of the party who were all anxiously looking their way. Aspen wondered if they all had known that Jenny was going to ask her out tonight. The thought settled nauseatingly in her stomach.

Aspen watched her return to their coworkers and other friends, then escaped to the bar. She had to be alone for a minute. How was she going to go back to work after this?

She felt like a jerk, even though she hadn't done anything wrong.

The bartender came to her and she ordered a water. She wanted to go home. Why didn't Vera just agree to come? Then this would never have happened. The thought made her angry, but just as quickly the anger fizzled into sadness. What was she doing wrong? Why did Vera keep her around if only to act like they weren't even dating?

As she took a sip from her glass of water, Aspen felt rather than saw two people sidle up on either side of her. Two men in similar crew-neck sweaters and tight business pants stood next to her. They asked the bartender for two beers, then the one with dark hair turned to her.

"Hey gorgeous," he said with a grin. "My buddy Nate saw you here. Thought we would come and say hello."

"Hello," Aspen said without a smile. She wondered if Jenny and the others could see her, or if she could signal to the bartender if things got out of hand.

"Let me buy you a drink," the blonde one said. He spoke softly, but it didn't make her any less uncomfortable.

Aspen gripped her water glass tighter. "I'm not drinking anymore tonight."

"Designated driver?" the other asked with a smirk. "Or

did you come here alone?"

I guess because you looked lonely sitting at the bar and it reminded me of how I felt. Aspen's voice died in her throat. But before she could respond that she was definitely not alone, no matter how it seemed, she felt a hand latch onto her arm and tug her out of her seat.

"Excuse me!"

She glanced at the voice and saw Vera's livid face before her. Aspen could hardly comprehend what she was seeing. Vera wore a short silver sequin dress, heels, and had a full face of makeup on. All Aspen could do was gape at her.

"How dare you steal my boyfriend!" Vera screeched in the most annoying, fake falsetto, pulling Aspen by the arm. The two men glanced at each other in alarm and silently backed away to give them space. "Don't deny it! I found out from Henry. He's outside right now. You're coming with me!"

Then Vera dragged Aspen stumbling out of the bar and into the parking lot, leaving the two perplexed men standing at the bar, eager to be left out of what they thought was a catty fight. Only once they reached her car did Vera stop and turn around.

"What the hell was that, Vera?" Aspen asked, slightly out of breath.

Vera crossed her arms. "You're welcome for saving you from those two creepy dudes."

Aspen rolled her eyes. "That was unnecessary."

"Why were you at the bar alone anyway? Where were Jenny and the others?" Vera asked.

Fear curdled in her stomach. "I actually went to the bar to escape her." She paused. "Jenny tried to ask me out. I had no idea she thought of me like that."

Vera stared at her. "What did you say?"

"No, of course!" Aspen looked at her in bewilderment. "What did you think I was gonna say?"

"I don't know! It's just that Jenny is so beautiful, and I know you guys are close at work…"

Aspen cocked her head. "Hold on a second. Are you jealous?"

"What? No." But Vera didn't look her in the eyes.

"Oh my god, you're jealous." Aspen nearly laughed out loud. "This whole time you've been jealous of *Jenny*. Is that why you never wanted to hang out with her?"

"It's not funny!" Vera sighed irritably. "I just thought there was no way you would want to be with me if you could be with someone like her." Aspen tried to interrupt but she held up a hand. "That first time we hung out with Jenny, I saw the way she looked at you. I knew it was only a matter of time before she asked you out. I thought you would want her instead of me. But now…"

"Vera, you should've just told me," Aspen said, half-angrily. "Why did you come here anyway? Did you come to make sure I wasn't dancing with her? Or maybe you just came to find a reason to break up with me."

"What?" Vera asked in disbelief.

"Let's face it, Vera. You say you want to be with me but then you act like you can hardly stand me. You're always busy, we never hang out with each other's friends, you won't visit me at my apartment—"

"Because I'm scared!" Vera cried out, and Aspen took a step back in surprise. "Aspen, I'm just gonna say it. I'm so in love with you it terrifies me. I'm scared that if we continue dating you'll get bored of me and choose someone like Jenny. So I made it seem like I wasn't interested because it would be easier to end things now than three years from now. But I still want you. I've always wanted you, so much it hurts. I want you in my life forever, Aspen. And I get if you need to talk about it—"

"No," Aspen said, cutting her off, and Vera sucked in a knife-like breath, "no more talking. All we do is talk." Then Aspen stepped forward and kissed her.

For a second Vera was frozen beneath her, but then she kissed her hungrily, wrapping her arms around Aspen's waist and pulling them flush against each other.

"Let's go back to my apartment," Aspen whispered without thinking when they broke apart, her eyes roaming down Vera's body from her green eyes to her long legs in shiny heels. She pinched the hem of Vera's dress, fingering the thin material that hardly covered any of her thighs. "What were you planning to do? Seduce me?"

Vera's chest still rose and fell from the kiss. "If I was, is it working?"

Aspen slid her hands to the small of Vera's back. "You have no idea," she said with a shake of her head, before kissing her again, their mouths meeting with more urgency this time.

Eventually they managed to stop kissing for long enough to get into Vera's car, though it was difficult for Aspen to resist pulling Vera's hand towards her.

Aspen ignored all her doubts and fears that Vera would change her mind the moment they entered her apartment, that this was all a dream that was too good to be true. The car ride to her apartment was silent save for the kisses Aspen left trailing up Vera's arm and on her neck.

At last Vera swerved into a parking spot on the side of the road. They hopped out of the car and Aspen eagerly led Vera up the steps and into her apartment. Once they were inside, Aspen turned and pushed Vera up against the door, kissing her deeply until Vera's hands tugged at the hem of her dress.

They looked at each other and nodded before heading back to Aspen's room. A flurry of questions whirled inside her mind. *What were they doing? What if she leaves again? What if I end up heartbroken?*

But all of these thoughts melted away like snow under the sun when Vera guided her onto the bed. Their lips met with a newfound passion that had never been there before, and a wild, almost painful longing cut deep inside of Aspen, reverberating down her legs and weakening her knees. Her hands trembled as she lifted Vera's dress above her shoulders.

Even though Aspen knew they would have to talk at some point, she didn't care. Not now. Not as long as Vera was kissing her and roaming her hands down her chest. Not when she has worked so hard to have Vera right here in front of her.

Aspen kissed Vera until her lips were sore and they fell asleep in each other's arms.

10

Layla woke up with a chill as a breeze from the sliver of open window passed over her skin. She could hear the water running in the bathroom. Zach was already awake. She threw off the covers and got up. Her lecture class started in two hours.

She was already dressed by the time Zach came out of the shower with a towel wrapped around his waist. She had on layers of thrifted jeans, sweaters, flannel, and scarves so that she looked more like a farmer than a fashion student.

She did a twirl. "The look is cottage cozy. Do you like it?"

He shrugged. "You look good in everything, Layla."

"Someone's in a bad mood," Layla said in surprise.

"Are you free later today?" Zach asked, ignoring her comment. This bothered her and she crossed her arms, not wanting to respond.

"Maybe. Why?"

Zach glanced at her but otherwise did not seem to notice her anger. "I thought you could swing by the studio. We can go out to dinner afterward. Just us."

"Like last time?" Layla asked tersely.

"What was wrong with last time?"

Layla huffed a laugh. "Oh I don't know. How about your whole band inviting themselves to our dinner? Or is that what you mean when you say *just us?*"

"Layla," Zach implored as he pulled his jeans on. "You have to understand that my bandmates are like family. Sometimes I can't say no to them."

"Well don't bother saying no to them tonight," Layla shot back, before turning around and grabbing her tote bag. "I'm busy."

"Busy? With who?"

Layla smiled. *"Just me."*

"Are you going to see that Will guy again?" Zach demanded.

"What, are you jealous?" she asked, raising a brow.

He scowled. "No. I just don't like that you're so close with your ex all of a sudden."

"What about you and Gianna?"

"That's not fair," Zach said with a roll of his eyes. "She's the lead singer of my band. I can't help seeing her."

"Exactly! You're always with her." Layla tried to hold

back her frustration but now that they were arguing it all wanted to come out. "I have to see you with her all the time and I hate it. You guys don't even act like exes half the time!"

Zach shook his head. "You're being dramatic, Layla."

"Dramatic? *You* started this by bringing up Will. Don't you dare make this about me."

"That's because I actually have a good reason," Zach argued, pointing at her. "You never mentioned Will before and now all of a sudden he comes to New York and you won't stop seeing him?"

"You know, I wasn't planning on seeing him again, but maybe now I will!" Then Layla stormed out of the apartment and hurried downstairs before Zach could stop her.

On the way to her subway station, she called Will, out of revenge or something else, she didn't know. Her hands were shaking and she could barely breathe. Tears filled her eyes but she refused to cry. After a few rings, Will picked up.

"Will?"

"Is everything okay?" he asked worriedly, hearing the tears in her voice.

"Yes," she said. "Well, no. Not really. I…I'm sorry about yesterday. Do you think maybe we could talk?

Zach and I just got into an argument and I have no one here that really understands me like you do. You're the only person I could talk to about this." Then she added hurriedly, "But if you don't want to see me again, I totally understand."

"No, of course, let's meet up," Will said quickly. "My flight only leaves tomorrow."

Layla felt a weight on her shoulders lighten at the thought of seeing him again, and she wiped her tears away. "Okay, great. My classes finish around three. Want to meet up afterward?"

She could almost hear his smile. "See you then."

Classes passed by in an agonizingly slow crawl through the early afternoon. Layla had to grab a coffee on her way to meet Will just to feel alive. She had offered to take him to The Met, which he hadn't visited yet.

Will was standing at the base of the steps in front of the museum. Crowds of tourists and museum-goers surged around him, his golden curls like a beacon of light amidst a sea of black winter coats.

Layla stopped a few steps away from him. He offered her a smile, then they walked up to the door together.

"So…you and Zach got in a fight?" Will asked hesitantly once they bought their tickets.

"Yes."

"Do you want to talk about it?"

Layla frowned. "Only if you would be okay with it."

"Of course," Will said, glancing at her with a wry smile. "Friends, right?"

"Friends." Layla nodded, then sighed as she prepared to recount the fight. "We actually fought over you. Sort of. He's jealous that I've been spending time with you. But when I brought up the fact that he used to date the lead singer of his band for four years, he calls *me* dramatic."

"Wait, Zach used to date the redhead?"

"Yep. But that's not the only thing that bothers me about him. Like the other day, he said he would take me out to sushi after his recording session, but then all of his bandmates invited themselves to *our* dinner. He didn't say no or anything, and the whole night they barely spoke to me."

Will's brows raised. "Wow. Does he do that often?"

"Zach will always pick his band over me," Layla said bitterly. "And I get it. It's for his career. I would choose fashion school commitments over him too. But I also make time for him outside of it, and he doesn't always do the same for me."

"This sounds like a bigger issue than just jealousy," Will said carefully.

"He also never compliments my outfits unless I ask him. And he doesn't like to have deep conversations. Sometimes I think he's just with me for…you know…"

"Ah." Will nodded his head slowly. "Can I say what I really think?"

"Of course," Layla said quickly.

"I think that he doesn't treat you right." He said it plain and simple, looking at her without a trace of doubt or resentment. Just the truth. "You deserve someone who loves you, who wants to be with you and spend time with you because of who you are as a person, not just because of looks or sex."

Layla stared at him, her head spinning. "Do you think I should break up with him?"

Will half-smiled. "That's not my decision to make. But I definitely think you should talk with him about it. Maybe if you tell him how you're truly feeling he will make the effort to change."

Her heart sank as she thought about telling Zach how she felt. She knew he would never listen to her. "In the beginning he wasn't like this," she said sadly. "He was very attentive and loving. I thought he would always be like that."

"It's not your fault if someone doesn't see your worth," Will said, his voice quiet.

"Thank you, Will." Layla took a deep breath and smiled at him. "So, do you want to see the Ancient Egyptian section?"

They strolled around the museum for the next few hours as if they had been good friends for years, laughing at each other's jokes and pointing out art pieces that interested them. Layla had never felt so light, and soon she even forgot about why she and Will had argued the day before.

As their museum visit came to an end, Layla asked, "So, your flight leaves tomorrow?"

"Yes," Will said with a sigh. "Back to Japan."

"You don't sound too excited."

He shrugged. "I am. I love it there. But like you, sometimes I miss my old life."

"Why don't you move back to California?" she asked.

"I don't know…" He glanced at her, then away. "Things have changed. I think moving back now would only make me realize that my old life is gone."

They were walking back towards Zach's apartment

now. It was like they were running out of time, even though she knew nothing could happen between them. Layla had the sudden urge to tell him everything she was feeling, all her doubts, her fears, about Zach, and about herself. Even about Will. *You were so in love.*

Maybe she still was.

"Will, I wanted to tell you something," Layla said before she lost her nerve.

"Yes?" he asked, his voice tense.

"I just wanted to say that when we broke up, it wasn't because…it wasn't because I didn't love you anymore." She glanced at him, then nearly lost her breath when she saw him looking back at her with a burning intensity. "I was scared. I was scared you would lose interest in me if we dated long-distance, and I wanted to protect myself. But it was never about you. I hope you know that."

Will nodded thoughtfully, his eyes now avoiding hers. They were only a few blocks away from Zach's apartment. She wondered if this was the last time she would see him.

"I always regretted that day," Will said. "Not because you ended things, but because I let you get away without a fight." He breathed in and then out. "But I'm glad you moved on. If you're happy, then I'm happy. And you can always consider me a friend."

Layla tried to ignore the disappointment she felt, and the screaming urge to cry and tell him that it wasn't true, that since the day they kissed, she had not stopped thinking about him, even after all these months apart.

Instead, she smiled. "Same here."

They had reached Zach's apartment. Layla's chest constricted. Will glanced up at the tall building with a strange look that she could not place, somewhere between longing and bitterness.

"I guess this is goodbye," Layla said with a nervous laugh.

Will looked at her, then suddenly he was hugging her, and Layla melted into his warm embrace. She wrapped her arms around him tightly, afraid that once she let go, she would never feel happy again.

"Goodbye, Layla," he whispered, then stepped away, forcing Layla to retract her arms.

She nodded quickly, not trusting her voice, but before she could try to respond he had turned and walked away. After watching him disappear around the corner, Layla headed inside, wondering how she was going to explain how she was feeling to Zach. But she stopped short when she opened the door to the empty apartment, and sighed.

Zach was already gone.

11

Aspen awoke to the smell of a familiar, flowery perfume. Her arms were wrapped around Vera's waist. She felt Vera try to gently move her arms, and Aspen instinctively tightened her hold, shaking her head.

"No," Aspen muttered, her voice groggy. "If I open my eyes, this might all be a dream. You might disappear."

Vera brushed her fingertips across the dip of Aspen's bare waist. "I'm not going anywhere, I promise. But we should eat something. And talk."

Aspen's eyes fluttered open and landed on Vera's face, her nose dotted with faint freckles that could only be seen up close. But she didn't loosen her grip on Vera, instead pulling her closer and kissing the crook of Vera's neck.

"Aspen," Vera said tenderly, "aren't you hungry? I can make us breakfast. And I have to put some clothes on. You too."

"Fine," Aspen relented with a groan. She leaned back, scanning Vera's face for any regret, but she only found a soft love in her green eyes. Very reluctantly, Aspen unwound her arms and got up.

Vera got out of bed after Aspen, wrapping a blanket around her bare skin. Aspen walked to her closet and rummaged through a pile of clothes until she grabbed a large hoodie.

"Here," she said, throwing the hoodie at Vera, who caught it in the air in surprise. "You can wear this."

Aspen grabbed a large T-shirt and sweatpants for herself. Vera had shrugged on the hoodie, which fell low enough to act like a dress.

"Just a hoodie, no pants?" Vera asked, eyeing the hem of the hoodie falling past the top of her thighs.

"Nope," Aspen said with a grin, grabbing the front of Vera's hoodie and pulling her in for another kiss. "And *I'm* going to make breakfast."

She led Vera by the hand into the kitchen, kissing her one last time before taking out eggs and bread. Vera sat at the counter and watched her heat up a frying pan on the stovetop.

"How do you want your egg?" she asked.

Vera smiled. "Sunny side up, please."

Aspen cracked both eggs into the pan, then slid two slices of bread into the toaster. "So…we should talk."

"Yeah."

"I'm not sure what to say," Aspen said honestly. "You said last night that you were scared I would get bored of you. Why would you think that?"

Vera fidgeted with the ends of the sweater. "We're just so different. We like different things. We have completely opposite personalities. I want to stay in, and I don't like hanging out with other people all the time. You like to party and have a bunch of friends. You want to *model,* Aspen. I'm studying engineering. We're living completely different lives."

"So?" Aspen turned around to butter the toast. "Want avocado?"

"Of course," Vera said, a laugh in her voice.

She cut open an avocado and layered some on each toast, then she scooped up the fried eggs and laid them on top. "Done. Here's yours. And salt and pepper."

Vera slid her plate closer. "This looks great, thank you."

They both took bites of their toast. Aspen busied herself with making coffee while Vera ate her food. Once the coffee was brewing, Aspen turned around and leaned on the counter, sighing deeply.

"Vera, look at me," Aspen said quietly. Vera glanced up at her in surprise. "I know it's hard to forget how I used to be, but I've changed a lot since high school. I don't party excessively. I don't get drunk all the time.

I have a job, an apartment, and a girlfriend that I fall more in love with every day. As for being different, well, don't you think that could be a good thing? It makes our relationship more interesting. And I love it. If I wanted to date someone like me, I would've gone for your sister."

"Aspen!"

"Kidding," she said with a cheeky grin.

"Hope so," Vera said.

Aspen took Vera's hands in hers. "I choose you because you bring out the best in me. I love the person I become with you. Is that so bad?"

Vera's eyes shined as she looked at Aspen. "No, it's not."

She squeezed Vera's hands. "It's okay to be scared. Believe me, I am too. I'm always wondering when you'll see that you're too good for me. But that's part of falling in love. You realize that the person who you let into your heart has the most power to break it, but instead of pushing them away, you bring them closer, because that's how much you trust them."

Vera looked down at her half-eaten toast. "I guess we're both being self-destructive when we think about possibilities in the future that haven't happened yet. I've just always thought of my future, and sometimes forget that I still have to live in the present."

"Is that why you don't want to move in?" Aspen asked.

Vera hopped out of her chair and walked around the kitchen counter. Aspen's eyes followed Vera helplessly as she came close, caging Aspen against the counter with her arms.

"I've been thinking…maybe it would be good for me to move in," Vera said. "I'd be able to focus more and be near you." Then she tilted her head to brush a kiss on Aspen's cheek, while Aspen's hands automatically circled Vera's waist.

"If that's what you want, then you'll need this," Aspen whispered, her hand reaching into her pocket and pulling out the spare keys she had slipped in there when Vera wasn't looking.

She dangled the keys in front of Vera's wide eyes before gently pulling Vera's left hand up and sliding the metal key ring on Vera's ring finger. Vera sucked in a small breath as the metal took the place where an engagement ring would be.

Aspen pressed a kiss on Vera's slightly parted mouth. Vera curled her arms around Aspen's neck and kissed her softly.

They didn't need to say words, not anymore, because Aspen could hear the promise anyway. Aspen was scared, she couldn't deny it. They both were. But that was part of falling in love.

It was always scariest just before the fall.

The sun sat above the ocean's horizon in a hot, orange glow, bathing the Santa Monica mountains in a hazy light. Aspen gazed at the familiar beach view and wondered if she would be able to live without it.

"Aspen!"

She turned. Vera was walking towards her, sandals in one hand and the other waving at her. Aspen grinned and ran towards her. Once they reached each other Aspen threw her arms around Vera, who let out a small scream and laughed when Aspen tried to twirl her around.

Aspen set her down, then took Vera's hand and led her toward the water. They both were silent for a moment. Even though Aspen had asked her to meet here after class, she didn't know how to start the conversation.

"So..." Vera began hesitantly, "what did you want to talk about? You said you had news?"

"Good news," Aspen said at once, and Vera relaxed slightly. "I got an email from a modeling agency that I applied to. They want me to come in and do an interview and everything. It would be a huge opportunity for me."

"Oh my god, Aspen, that's amazing!" Vera exclaimed,

looking at her in shock. "Why did you make it sound so ominous?"

"Well, because it's in New York," Aspen said quietly. "New York City."

Vera stopped mid-step and stared at her. "Oh."

"Yeah." Aspen kicked the sand with her feet, her face aflame and her chest tight. She glanced at Vera's stricken face and added, "But I won't accept it if you don't want me to."

"Are you kidding?" Vera demanded. "You have to accept it. You're going to fly out for the interview, right? When is it?"

"I said I could fly out tomorrow morning," Aspen said, her eyes pricking with tears. "And in the application, I said I could start working immediately."

Vera looked at her in mingling love and sadness. "I'm so happy for you, Aspen."

"That's why I wanted to talk." Aspen took in a deep breath before she continued. "I'm scared you won't want to do long distance."

"Right." Vera avoided her gaze, looking off toward the horizon instead. "That would be a big change."

Aspen's heart sunk, but she tried to smile. "We don't have to think about it right now. I still have to get accepted."

"You're going to get accepted, Aspen," Vera said sadly. "I know it. They would be stupid not to. We already tried long-distance, and you know how difficult it is. But you can't throw away your career for me."

"What are you saying then?" Aspen asked tersely. "You'd want to break up?"

Vera bit her lip, her eyes watering. "I don't know, Aspen." Her voice was hardly a whisper as she tried to hold back tears. "It would be hard, that's all."

"Not like it's been easy with both of us here."

"Then imagine how it will be if you're on the other side of the country," Vera said bitterly.

Aspen glared at her. "That's not what I meant and you know it."

A tear rolled down Vera's cheek and Aspen reached out to brush it away. "Maybe we shouldn't rush into things if you're going away."

"It's too late for that," Aspen said wryly. "We already decided to move in together."

Vera shook her head with a small smile. "Have you told Layla yet?"

"No, I wanted to tell you first."

"Have you bought your flight? Where are you going to stay? And for how long?" Vera asked the question one after the other, as though she were Aspen's mother and not her girlfriend.

Aspen couldn't help but laugh. "Whoa, no need to panic. I have it all figured out. I'm staying with Layla in her dorm for three days. I'll book my flight when we get back home."

Vera took Aspen's hand firmly. "I do support you, Aspen. Whatever decision you make, I support you."

"I know," Aspen said, smirking. She kissed Vera's cheek. "That's why I love you."

"And I love you."

Aspen looked down at her phone. She was on the right block, but she couldn't tell which building she was supposed to enter. Someone bumped her shoulder and she muttered a sorry as she looked up.

Then she saw her. Layla was walking a few yards away and heading right towards her. Aspen continued walking until they nearly crossed paths before calling out Layla's name.

Layla stifled a scream, stopping in her tracks and staring at Aspen in bewilderment for a few seconds before she let out an excited squeal, running straight towards her.

"Aspen! You're here!" she exclaimed before engulfing

Aspen in a tight hug. "I've missed you so much."

Aspen laughed as Layla hugged her so hard she could barely breathe. "I'm not leaving yet! Save this for the goodbye."

Layla stepped back, her eyes shining with happiness. "I'm so glad you're here." She took a deep breath. "I'm breaking up with Zach."

12

spen stared at her, her mouth open. She quickly closed it and looked around as if worried someone had overheard. "What? When did you decide this?"

Layla forced a smile. "I think I knew for a while. He wasn't treating me well. You were right. I don't love him. And I shouldn't be with someone just for validation."

Aspen eyed her curiously. "Did you see Will?"

"Maybe."

"Ah, I see." Aspen smirked, looping an arm through hers. "So this has *nothing* to do with that almost kiss?"

Layla's heart clenched. "I wish," she muttered. "But Will has clearly moved on. Somehow I still haven't. Besides, he leaves for Japan today, so it doesn't matter if I wanted it or not."

"When are you breaking up with Zach?" Aspen asked.

"Tonight." Layla sighed just thinking about it. "He has a gig somewhere that I said I couldn't go to. But now I think I'll stop by after his set is done and end it. I would wait until he gets home but I don't want to lose my nerve. Besides, I've already packed up my things from his apartment."

"Wow, that's pretty official." Aspen shook her head. "Well, what are we going to do until then?"

Layla smiled and led her into her dorm building. "I thought we could go shopping in Soho."

Aspen squealed. "I've missed shopping with you!"

They took the elevator up to the fifth floor, where her dorm room was the second door on the right. The hallways were cramped and the rooms were old but there was still a certain New York charm to them that Layla loved.

"Aw, your room is so cute!" Aspen looked around the small dorm room which was in a state of chaos after bringing back half her closet from Zach's place.

"Sorry it's such a mess."

Aspen dragged her by the hand until they were both on her bed. "We both know I'm messier than you." She latched onto Layla and snuggled closer. "Guess who gets to cuddle me tonight?"

Then Layla felt Aspen's fingers tickling her ribs and she screeched, kicking her as she twisted away, though she couldn't get rid of the grin on her face. "Aspen, stop it!"

"Sorry," Aspen said with a smile that did not seem sorry

at all. "I just miss having my best friend around to annoy."

Layla raised a brow. "Don't you annoy Vera now? How's that going by the way?"

"I'm not sure," Aspen said, her smile fading. "I didn't tell you this, but there's another reason I'm visiting New York."

She went still. "What?"

"I got asked by a modeling agency here to do an interview." Aspen looked at her with barely contained joy. "I wanted to surprise you."

Layla could hardly believe it. She screamed and tackled Aspen onto the bed. "Oh my god! Oh my god! We're gonna be roommates! Oh my god! This is the best news ever!"

Aspen bit her lip, and Layla calmed down, sitting cross-legged beside her. "Which means I leave Vera, and we'll have to date long-distance."

All at once the excitement rapidly disappeared as she thought of what Vera must be feeling. "Did you guys talk about it?" she asked.

"Barely," Aspen said quietly, looking down at her hands fiddling in her lap. "She wasn't sure it would work. She was scared we would both be too busy."

"And you?" Layla pressed. "What do you think?"

Aspen looked at her brokenly. "I don't know."

Layla ran a soothing hand down Aspen's back. "It'll be alright. You guys can survive this, I know it."

"But anyways," Aspen said quickly, smiling brightly, though her eyes still gleamed with unshed tears. "I'm here to comfort *you*. Whatever you need, you got me."

"Thank you, Aspen." Layla took her hand and squeezed. "You're the best friend ever—"

She smirked. "I know."

"—besides when you decided to date my sister."

Aspen groaned.

After a long day of shopping, where Layla bought too many clothes she didn't need, and a fun dinner constantly laughing at each other's jokes, Aspen returned to her dorm room while Layla trekked to Midtown where Zach had a showing.

She felt bad leaving Aspen alone, but Aspen insisted that she was fine since she had to go to bed early anyway for her interview tomorrow morning.

Layla ignored the racing of her heart and the dampness on her neck as the subway cart rattled and screeched its way north beneath the city. She wondered if this was a mistake, but then she recalled her conversation with Will.

It's not your fault if someone doesn't see your worth.

All too soon the subway arrived at her stop. She took in a deep breath and exited the station, the brisk evening air greeting her upon ascending from the warmth of the underground.

Zach's show was at a private party on the penthouse floor of a fancy-looking building. A hired bouncer stood at the door beside the doorman. He filtered who could enter the party, but she knew her name was on the list.

Sure enough, once she said she was here for the party, the bouncer checked her ID and something on his phone before nodding silently and escorting her to the elevator, where he used a special key card to send her to the penthouse. The elevator ride felt like an eternity as each floor passed with a soft *ding.*

Soon the elevator slowed to a stop at the top floor. She could already hear music pulsing through the walls before the doors slid open and revealed the glossy interior of a sparsely decorated, modern apartment filled with well-dressed guests spilling out onto a balcony over a commanding view of the city. She knew the band would probably be somewhere near the balcony and headed in that direction.

She scooted her way through the crowds, politely de-clining a server holding a tray of drinks. The people were packed in the closer she got to the balcony, and many of them were dancing. At last Layla made it to the front.

Zach wasn't there.

In fact, none of the band members were hanging around and a new band had already started their set. An unfamiliar face belted out lyrics, and she did not recognize the guitarist, drummer, or bass player. Layla wondered whether Zach and the others had already left. She found that hard to believe, since Zach rarely missed an opportunity to party.

She grudgingly maneuvered her way back into the house and searched for a kitchen or spare room that looked like it might be used for the band members. In a dark hallway deeper inside the house Layla thought she saw a swish of red hair.

"Gianna!"

After a beat, the red-headed singer strutted out on black high-heeled boots. When she saw Layla, her eyes narrowed. "You're not supposed to be here."

Layla's heart pounded. "Zach invited me."

"Yes, but he said you weren't coming," Gianna said, placing a hand on her hip. "You should go."

"Why?" Layla was starting to feel angry. "Where is he?"

Gianna's eyes flickered to her left hesitantly. "Please leave, Layla."

It was the first time she had ever heard Gianna say her name. Layla's chest tightened as she brushed past a protesting Gianna and saw that she had glanced at a closed door behind her. Layla hardly hesitated before opening the door.

Her brain took a moment to process what she saw. Inside the room, sprawled on a large guest bed, was Zach. He was locked in an embrace with a woman Layla had never seen before, a brunette with a half-shrugged-off dress. They broke apart at the sound of the door opening and Zach scrambled away when he saw it was her.

Behind her, Gianna sighed. "It seems some habits never die."

"What are you doing here, Layla?" Zach asked, ignoring Gianna. He still had a smear of lipstick on his mouth, which Layla had always found endearing when it was hers. Now she found it pathetic. The other girl avoided Layla's glare and awkwardly pulled the straps of her dress back on her shoulders.

Layla drew herself tall, crossing her arms. "I was actually here to break up with you. And you just made it *much* easier."

With that, she turned on her heel and left the room. As she stormed down the hall, Layla nearly ran into Mateo, who grabbed her arms to stop her.

"Hey, hey, where are you—" He glanced behind her, his eyes widening. "Oh shit. I'm sorry, Layla."

"You knew?" Layla shook her head, her eyes stinging with tears. "You knew he was cheating on me and you didn't tell me?"

Mateo was silent, looking at the floor ashamed.

Layla shrugged off his hands. "God, I was so *stupid.*"

She heard Zach call out her name. Serenity poked her head out of another room after hearing the commotion, her eyes filled with surprise and then regret when she saw Layla. Layla ignored them all, shoving past Mateo and heading back to the elevators.

"Layla wait!" Zach called after her. "Let me explain!"

"Explain what?" she asked harshly, turning around.

He stood across from her in a hastily dressed shirt that she could tell was inside-out. Layla rolled her eyes. "Come on, Layla. It was a mistake. Please. I love you."

"Clearly not enough." Layla took a step closer and lowered her voice. "But it's okay, Zach. I understand. Seeing Will again made me realize that I deserve *so* much more. The only difference is that I was waiting until *after* breaking up with you to kiss him."

She lingered just to see the defiance and jealousy pass across his face before whirling around and leaving. Once she was in the elevator she allowed herself to breathe, sagging against the cold metal wall in exhaustion. She noticed belatedly that the tears were already streaming down her face.

Instead of taking the subway, Layla ordered a ride back to her dorm. She didn't have the heart to cry in public.

The ride passed in a blur, and before she knew it the car rolled to a stop in front of her dorm building. Layla hurried up to the third floor and with shaky hands unlocked the door to her room.

Aspen lifted her head sleepily from the bed. "Layla? Is it done?"

Layla nodded her head numbly. "He was cheating on me. Ironic, isn't it?"

Her eyes widened, and without a word, Aspen opened her arms. Layla let the sobs roll through her as she climbed into bed and curled up beside Aspen.

Within a few minutes, the exhaustion of the last few days weighed on her eyelids and lulled her into a deep, dreamless sleep.

13

Aspen woke up early to get dressed and eat breakfast before heading to the modeling agency for her interview. Luckily, it was located in the Flatiron District, which was a short subway ride away from Layla's dorm, who had class and therefore couldn't accompany her.

She chose a fitted, plain tank and jeans with a pair of short heels, then bundled up in one of Layla's puffer jackets. It took her a few minutes to orient herself once she emerged from the underground, but she soon found the building of the agency and entered with as much confidence as she could muster.

The secretary at the front desk led her upstairs to a spacious office where an older woman with a gray bob and glasses jotted notes on a pad of paper. She glanced up when Aspen entered the room and smiled.

"Ah, you must be here for the interview," she said in a deep voice with a thick French accent. "Come, take a seat. Aspen, right?"

Aspen sat nervously on the seat the woman pointed to. "Yes. Thank you for taking the time to meet with me, Ma'am."

"You may call me Miss Lavigne," she said, shaking Aspen's hand.

"It's nice to meet you, Miss Lavigne."

"So tell me, Miss Aspen, what experience do you have modeling?"

"I have mostly done social media posts for local brands," Aspen said, trying not to sound embarrassed at how little experience she had.

Miss Lavigne nodded, writing down something on the pad of paper. "Very good, very good. And for how long have you modeled? Tell me a bit more about your experiences."

"I've been modeling for over two years now. I was first approached by a clothing store in high school to model some of their clothes on social media. From there I got a few more requests. After graduating, I applied for agencies, and in the meantime I've been working as an assistant for an agency in Los Angeles."

After taking a few more notes, Miss Lavigne set the notepad down and folded her hands on the table in front of her. "Okay, *bien*. And why do you want to be a model? Why not, I don't know, go to college, study something, say, medicine or perhaps literature?"

"I actually didn't want to be a model growing up," Aspen said honestly. "Only once I did my first photo shoot did I fall in love with it. The camera flashing, trying different poses, bringing personality into the shots, I love all of it. During those shoots, time would slow down, and all I could focus on was that moment. In many ways, modeling brings me peace."

Miss Lavigne looked at her with a gentle smile. "Beautiful. Beautiful words from a beautiful girl. Of course, modeling is not easy, as you know. Some shoots will be hard, uncomfortable, and long. But if you love it, that is half the battle. Now can you get up and do a little walk here? Back and forth?"

Aspen dutifully stood up and walked carefully between the two walls of the office space. She remembered the techniques she learned and hoped it would be enough. Miss Lavigne held up her hand and Aspen came to a stop.

Miss Lavigne stood up. "Thank you. Those are all the questions I have for you, Miss Aspen. We will be in touch with you soon."

Then Aspen said her goodbyes and was escorted back downstairs and out into the bustling, noisy crowds of New York City.

After Layla got out of class, Aspen picked her up and they spent the rest of the day walking through Central Park before eating dinner at a pizza spot near her dorm room. Aspen swore the pizza was the best she ever had, which made Layla laugh.

She had never felt so weightless. Her life in Los Angeles had always felt like a burden to bear, but here her dreams of being a model seemed to be close enough to touch. The only missing piece to make the dream complete was Vera, but for now Aspen pushed the thought away.

Layla also looked happier, though she had cried throughout the night after breaking up with Zach. But she was smiling now as they walked back to her dorm.

"It's good to see you smiling," Aspen said.

"It's good to be free!" Layla skipped ahead and twirled as if she might break out into a dance. "No boys to worry about."

"What about Will?"

Layla came to a stop. "What about him?"

"I thought maybe you were breaking up with Zach to get back together with Will," Aspen said hesitantly. She didn't want to start a fight, but Layla only shrugged.

"It doesn't really matter, does it?" She smiled sadly.

"He's probably already in Japan."

"You could call him."

"There's no point," Layla said in a clipped voice. "What's meant to be will be. You know, *you're* one to talk. Have you spoken with Vera yet?"

Aspen's stomach turned. "I was going to call her tonight."

Layla's eyes softened. She placed a gentle hand on Aspen's arm. "She loves you, Aspen. I know you will make it work. Besides, you'll see her again before you know it."

I do support you, Aspen. Whatever decision you make, I support you.

But would that be enough when the time came? Or would Vera be too scared to commit if they didn't live in the same city?

These doubts followed Aspen back to Layla's dorm. While Layla was in the shower, Aspen called Vera, who picked up on the first ring as though she had been waiting for it. Vera's face appeared on her screen. A hoodie was pulled over her head and the room around her was dark and grainy, as if she had been watching TV. She heard the distant cars and noise of LA traffic.

"You look comfy," Aspen said with a fond smile. Her heart suddenly ached at the sight, as if they were already living long distance and Aspen missed her more than words.

Vera smiled. "How's New York?"

"It's amazing! Layla and I shopped in Soho and walked in Central Park. I had the best pizza today too and—"

"What about the interview?" Vera interrupted.

Aspen went silent, looking away from Vera's expectant face. Then she sighed. "It went well, I guess."

"Be honest," Vera pressed.

"Okay fine," Aspen muttered. "I spoke to this French lady who was really nice. But I still haven't heard back from them."

"You will," Vera said with more confidence than Aspen felt. Her chest squeezed at the thought of receiving that phone call. "Hey, Aspen."

"Yes?"

Vera had a strange look on her face. "Enjoy New York," she said after a pause. "We'll see each other again before you know it."

Aspen paused. It was the same thing Layla had said to her. She looked at Vera again, and for the first time she noticed that Vera was not, in fact, sitting in her room in the dark, but outside.

"Where are you?" Aspen asked.

The camera panned above Vera's head to tall buildings

checkered with lit-up windows. Aspen heard honks and distant sirens that she could hear outside her window. Then the camera swung around to show Layla's very familiar dorm building. "Are you going to let me in or what?"

Aspen's heart raced as she scrambled to the window and looked down at the sidewalk. She saw Vera waving below with one hand, the other holding her phone.

Vera laughed. "Surprise!"

"She's here?" Layla asked from behind her.

Aspen turned around. "You knew!"

Layla smirked. "Go get your girlfriend."

Without another word, Aspen ran out of the room, skipping the elevator and taking the stairs instead. Vera was shivering on the other side of the glass doors without a coat. When Aspen opened the door, Vera ran inside and barreled into Aspen, hugging her tightly.

"I can't believe you're here," Aspen whispered, surprised to find tears in her eyes. "Aren't you missing school?"

"A day," Vera said with a giddy laugh. "I told my professors that my sister was having surgery. But I have to leave early morning on Thursday."

"How are we going to fit in Layla's room?" Aspen asked, still holding onto Vera as if she might disappear if she let go.

"I used the last of my summer tutoring money to buy a hotel room for us," Vera said with a sly smile. "Consider it an apology for the last few months."

Aspen couldn't help but kiss her, tangling her hands in Vera's hair. "You don't need to apologize. For anything."

"So, should we go see Layla?" Vera asked, absentmindedly tucking a strand of Aspen's hair behind her ear. Her eyes were bright and her cheeks flushed, so that she looked the most alive Aspen had seen her in a long time.

Aspen shook her head. "You're amazing, do you know that?"

Vera took Aspen's hand in hers, her thumb caressing her knuckles tenderly. "Only for you."

14

L ayla hesitated at the door of her room, looking at Vera and Aspen who sat innocently at the edge of her bed, waiting for her to leave.

"You two will be okay while I'm gone?" Layla asked. "My classes will be done by dinner. We are still on for dinner, right?"

"Of course!" Vera nodded. "We'll probably do some sightseeing."

Aspen smirked, leaning into Vera. "We'll be fine. Trust me."

Layla crossed her arms. "Don't do anything in my room that you wouldn't want me seeing. You have your hotel room for that."

"We wouldn't dare," Aspen said sweetly, earning her a light shove from Vera. "Like you said, we have our hotel room for that."

"I'm leaving," Layla said with a roll of her eyes, though her heart warmed seeing her sister and best friend happy once more. She hadn't seen them so giddy since they first got together the summer after she and Aspen graduated. Now she could only hope it lasted.

Her commute to class was quick but miserable as rain began to pour unexpectedly. Layla rummaged in her tote bag and realized she had forgotten her umbrella. *Great.* She still hadn't gotten used to how often it rained here.

Even though Vera and Aspen's arrival was helping her forget about breaking up with Zach and learning that he cheated on her, Layla couldn't ignore the pain and embarrassment it caused her once she was in class with only another tedious lecture to distract her from depressing thoughts.

The hours dragged on with no hope in sight. Though her friends tried to lighten the mood and make her laugh during their break at a local café, by the time she left class it was all Layla could do not to start crying right then and there.

It wasn't sadness, exactly, or even anger at Zach. Not anymore. Sadness she had felt when she realized she wanted to end her relationship with Zach, anger she had felt when she learned that he had been cheating on her, but now all she felt was a deep-cutting disappointment.

Disappointment in herself, mainly, that she had ever allowed herself to fall for a man like Zach, but also disappointment in her life. Layla had hoped that in college she would meet the perfect man to replace Will and she would be swept off her feet, the rest of her life falling into place. Instead, love had never felt more far away, and New York City seemed dreary and cold rather than bustling and romantic.

She tried to sniffle the tears away as she walked from campus back to her dorm room, huddling under her jacket which did nothing to shield her from the rain. Her hair was already wet and she tried to bundle her tote bag in her arms so her textbooks wouldn't share the same fate.

Her dorm building was only one more block away. She was almost there. Half a block now. A few more steps—

"Layla!"

The voice stopped Layla in her tracks. Her heart skipped a beat. It was impossible, and yet…

"Layla, wait!"

She turned around in disbelief. "Will?"

Will stood across from her, standing beneath an umbrella, though his hair was wet on his forehead, the curls dripping, as if he had been caught in the downpour before he could find cover.

"Will, what are you doing here?" Layla asked, forgetting for a moment that the rain was pouring down on her.

"Here," Will said, stepping close to her and lifting the umbrella above the two of them. He looked down at Layla with a half-smile. "Happy to see me?"

"I thought you left," Layla whispered, her head spinning.

"I couldn't leave," Will said, shaking his head. "I delayed my flight."

Layla wanted to shake him. "Why?"

"I couldn't leave like that."

"But *why*, Will?" Layla tried to read the thoughts in his face and failed. "Why are you here? Speak, Will!"

"Because I needed to tell you something," Will said suddenly, then he shut his eyes tightly as if he couldn't face her and speak the words at the same time. "I couldn't leave until I told you how I felt. About you. About us. And I know you have a boyfriend, and I don't expect you to break up with him for me, but I know I would treat you better." He opened his eyes and looked at her brokenly. "I love you, Layla. I never stopped loving you. And no matter where I traveled or what I did I couldn't escape you. I knew if I didn't tell you, I would regret it for the rest of my life. So I'm not sorry, even if you hate me for it."

Layla stared at him, his shoulders stiff as if bracing for her answer. *I love you, Layla. I never stopped loving you.*

Her arms moved as if they were not hers, circling his neck right before she kissed him. Will stood still, unmoving beneath her touch. She stepped away hesitantly, but then Will grabbed her waist and pulled her in for another kiss. He kissed her cheeks and neck feverishly as they broke apart, even when the umbrella leaned to the side and the rain pelted on their faces.

"Zach?" Will asked breathlessly between kisses.

Layla smirked. "I already broke up with him."

"What?" He pulled back and tried to turn a grin into a frown. "I'm sorry."

She laughed. "I'm not. I caught him cheating on me the same night I decided to break up with him."

"What a loser," Will said viciously. "He didn't deserve you."

"He didn't," Layla said, standing up on her tiptoes so that their lips brushed. Will's lashes lowered as he waited, holding his breath. "But you do." Then she kissed him again, winding her fingers through his curls as she used to love, tugging at one until he smiled against her mouth.

"God, I missed this," Will murmured.

"No. *Way*. Is that Will?"

Layla scrambled away from Will at the voice, her cheeks burning as she turned and saw Vera and Aspen standing in front of her dorm building, huddled under the same umbrella, and looking right at them. Vera raised a brow and Aspen smirked.

"I didn't know you were still in town," Vera said, but she spoke in a teasing tone, and Layla relaxed a little.

Aspen gave Layla a knowing look. "I guess there'll be four of us at dinner then?"

Layla glanced at Will questioningly, who grinned. She couldn't help but smile too. "If you two don't mind?"

"Of course not," Vera said, rather offended. "Will was my friend *first,* remember?"

"Let's not get into that discussion," Aspen muttered, and all of them laughed as they walked together towards the restaurant.

After Will hugged Vera and Aspen and caught them up on the last few days, he agreed to meet with them tomorrow for lunch to fully catch up while Layla was in class. Then for the rest of the walk, Will hung back with Layla, both of them crouched under his umbrella and holding hands.

"It's like nothing's changed," Will said quietly, motioning towards Aspen and Vera. He was surely remembering the many double dates they had gone on during the summer before Aspen and Vera took a break. It felt like a lifetime ago.

"So…you delayed your flight?" Layla asked awkwardly.

"Yes. I leave for Japan the day after tomorrow," Will said, glancing at her. "My parents think I have an interview at NYU."

"What do they say about you going to college here?"

Will shrugged. "They just want me to be happy."

"Are you?"

"I am now," Will said with a grin, his hand tightening on hers. "It'll be hell going back, though."

"You must love it there," Layla protested.

"I do. But it's not the same. It doesn't always feel like home."

"What if you don't go to a school in New York?" Layla asked. It sounded like a test, but she didn't want to scare him. "I mean, what other schools are you considering?"

"Some in California," Will said slowly. "But my top choice is Columbia."

They had reached the restaurant. Vera and Aspen checked in with the host and in a few minutes, their waiter would escort them to their table.

Layla turned to Will, who looked at her as if he wanted to say something.

"Layla, I—"

"Guys!" Aspen called out to them, waving a hand. "Come on."

Will smiled tightly. "It's nothing. We can talk about it later."

Layla nodded, forcing a smile, though her heart sank. *What were they going to do now?* She thought kissing Will would solve all her problems, but now it felt like it had just complicated them.

But as they sat down to their table, Will's hand finding hers once more, for the first time Layla felt like the world was back to normal again.

<h1 align="center">15</h1>

Aspen rolled over in bed and opened her eyes. Vera slept soundly beside her, the bed sheet slipping off her bare shoulders.

After dinner, they dropped Layla off at her dorm before returning to the hotel. It was amusing to see Will and Layla sneak glances at each other and blush when they were caught. While Aspen was happy that her best friend and Will might reunite, she was worried it would only result in more heartbreak.

Once she and Vera returned to the hotel room, they stayed up watching the National History Channel and cuddling in their bed, though she can hardly remember what they saw. Aspen had been over the moon all night, and she could not think of a better start to her morning.

"I can feel you staring at me," Vera mumbled. She grabbed Aspen's arm and pulled her closer, giving Aspen a light kiss before curling up against her.

Aspen grinned. "Sleepy?"

Vera rolled her eyes. "Tired. You snored all night."

"I don't snore!"

This started a brief tousle that ended in Aspen straddling Vera and trailing kisses down her neck. Vera arched into her touch, gently tugging at Aspen's hair as she traced a line down her stomach with her mouth, spreading Vera's legs open with a gentle grip on her thighs.

For the rest of the morning Aspen lay curled up in Vera's arms in a hazy sleep of bliss. After what felt like a peaceful eternity, Vera's phone buzzed with a text, and she reached out to grab it.

"Shoot, it's almost noon. We should start getting ready," Vera said with a sigh, sitting up. "We told Will we'd get lunch, remember?"

Aspen stretched her arms. "We should do this more often. Just us two, waking up together, with nothing to do all morning..."

"Isn't that what your apartment is for?" Vera asked playfully as she swung her legs over the side of the bed. "Just us two?"

"Until I move," Aspen said quietly.

Vera paused, her hands holding a pair of pants. She glanced at Aspen curiously. "How do you feel about moving?"

"I hate it." Aspen covered her face to hide the tears that

threatened to rise. "I don't want to leave you. I don't want to risk losing you because of it."

"You won't lose me," Vera said softly.

Aspen looked at her through her fingers. Vera had a small smile on her face. "No?"

"No." Vera pulled on the pants along with a shirt and sweater before crawling across the bed and taking Aspen's hands in hers. She stared deeply into Aspen's eyes. "I promise I won't give up. Even if you move halfway across the world, I won't give up on us. We have to try and make this work. We owe it to ourselves."

"What if you meet someone at UCLA? Or we can't see each other that often because we're busy?" Aspen asked worriedly, the tears falling down her face.

Vera kissed her cheeks where the tears fell. "It won't matter, because I love you."

"I love you too."

"Besides," Vera added brightly, "if we make it through four years, I can apply to graduate schools where you live. And if we make it through that, well, there's not much that can stop us, right?"

Aspen stared at her, and Vera glanced away with a blush. They had never really spoken explicitly that far into the future, and Aspen's heart beat clumsily at the thought of all those changes in her life. But if she had

Vera at her side, they didn't seem as daunting anymore.

"I don't think I could live without you," Aspen said honestly.

Vera looked at her, then smiled so happily that Aspen wanted to cry even more. "I really want to kiss you, but I know if I do, I'll never stop."

With that, she dragged Aspen off the bed and they finished getting dressed—only pausing when Aspen tried to kiss her again, causing another wrestling match that ended in even more kissing—and only managing to leave the hotel thirty minutes after noon.

As they walked into the bright sunlight gleaming across the city, at last Aspen knew everything was going to be alright.

They met Will outside a Ramen restaurant that served good bubble tea. Vera hugged him hard, and Aspen realized they hadn't seen each other for several months.

While Vera had remained friends with Will after his break up with Layla—albeit with a new awkwardness that hadn't been there before—Aspen on the other hand had taken the role of Layla's best friend and didn't speak with him again. But since Vera was still friends with him and now he and Layla might be getting back together, Aspen figured she could be civil.

She wondered briefly what would happen if she and Vera ever broke up. While Layla never stopped being her friend through their first break up, since the day Layla found out about their relationship, Aspen had known that if it came down to it, Layla would always side with her sister. Sometimes she feared that if they broke up again, she would lose not one but two of the people she loved most in this world. But she supposed that was the price she had to pay to date her best friend's sister.

"So…" Vera began after they sat down and ordered. "What's going on with you and Layla?"

Will blushed. "I'm not sure."

"You're not sure?" Aspen asked pointedly. "Well, I'm sure I saw you two kissing. What's that about?"

Vera nudged her not-so-discreetly. "What Aspen's trying to ask is are you two back together?"

"No!" Will exclaimed in alarm, then cleared his throat. "I mean, it's a difficult situation."

"Layla told me you moved on and don't have feelings for her anymore," Aspen said, feeling the need to defend Layla in her absence. "Is that true?"

Will looked positively embarrassed now, much to Aspen's delight. "She had a boyfriend. I didn't want to make things more complicated."

"So you do still love her!" Vera said, clapping her hands.

"Who knew you were such a romantic," Aspen muttered, and Vera rolled her eyes.

"But it doesn't matter," Will said quickly, and they both looked at him, startled. "I'm going back to Japan tomorrow morning, and Layla lives in New York now. What if I go to school in California and not New York? What if I don't even go to college and I stay in Japan for another year? Are we going to date long-distance? I don't even know if Layla *wants* to get back together, let alone date someone halfway across the world."

The words reminded Aspen of her conversation with Vera, and sure enough, when she turned, Vera was looking right back at her. She had a small smile on her face, perhaps remembering the promises they had made to each other.

"You two are like a married couple," Will said with a laugh. "You're reading each other's minds already."

"You know, Aspen is moving to New York too," Vera said. "She got offered a modeling job here."

"I got *interviewed,*" Aspen hastily corrected. "But yes, I might be moving to the Big Apple and rooming with Layla."

Will's eyes widened. "That's…Wow. Congrats!"

"It's a big change," Vera continued slowly, "not only for Aspen but for us as well. We'll be dating long-distance for at least the next few years, if not longer. It's not easy, but if you want to be with that person, sometimes you have to make sacrifices."

"But it's different for you two," Will said, catching on to what Vera was implying. "You guys have been dating for longer. And—and you guys love each other. So much. I've never seen two people so perfect for one another."

"Thank you, Will," Vera said with a half-smile. "That means a lot. But even we have our moments."

"You should've seen our last fight," Aspen added wryly, earning another not-so-subtle shove from Vera. "What? It's true."

"What we're *trying* to say," Vera said, turning back to Will, "is that every relationship requires sacrifices. But the only way to get through those tough times is to communicate."

"In other words," Aspen drawled, "go talk with her."

"What if she says no?" Will asked hesitantly.

Vera and Aspen shared a look, before Vera smiled and said, "Then you move on. But the question is…"

"…what if she says *yes*?" Aspen finished, finding Vera's hand already open underneath the table, waiting for her to hold.

16

Layla looked at herself in the mirror, twisting to get a better angle. She wore a long red velvet skirt and a black knit sweater with tall boots. Once she shrugged on her long black coat, she felt distinctly New York. She looked good, but she was still nervous. Would *he* like it? What if this was a mistake? What if he regretted seeing her again?

A message from Will on her phone momentarily distracted her.

Will: *I'm here.*

Layla took a deep breath in, fixing the strands of hair around her face and rechecking her makeup for the thousandth time. It wasn't as if Will hadn't seen her without makeup before or in nothing but a ratty t-shirt, but that was a long time ago. What if he didn't like how much she had changed since then?

Soon she could delay no more. Layla took the elevator down, trying to force her heartbeat to a regular rhythm, but to no avail. She saw Will on the street and her throat constricted. He looked so handsome in his usual sweater and jeans, his copper curls falling over his brow as he braced himself against a cold wind.

He straightened up when he saw her walk outside. "Layla," he said quietly, looking at her with a small smile. "You look beautiful."

"Thank you," she said, blushing. "And you look handsome."

Will held out his hand which Layla hadn't noticed was holding a full bouquet of red roses behind his back. "These are for you."

"You didn't have to," Layla said, taking the flowers carefully. "It's not like it's our first date or anything."

"No," Will said. "It means more this time."

Layla glanced at him in surprise, but he showed no sign of awkwardness, his eyes bright and firmly on her. He held out his hand when she didn't respond, and she took it, a rush running through her head when they touched.

They walked side by side down the street to a nearby Italian restaurant. Layla had never been before, but Will said they had good reviews. From what she saw online, it looked fancy.

"So this *is* a date then?" Layla asked, raising a brow.

"I want it to be," Will said sincerely, then hesitated. "Do

you?"

Layla smiled. "Yes, I do."

The restaurant was indeed fancy, with plush leather booths along the wall and candlelit tables covered in white cloth. A waiter directed them to their booth and handed them menus.

"How was lunch with Aspen and Vera?" Layla asked, if only to start the conversation.

"It was fun. They look happy together." Will paused. "I heard Aspen's moving to New York. How do you feel about that?"

"I would love to live in an apartment with Aspen, but I worry how she and Vera will do with long-distance." Layla avoided his eyes. "It's difficult to keep up with a relationship through phone calls and texts. After a while, one of you might get bored, or find someone new, or just fall out of love."

"Do you think that will happen?" Will asked, looking at her meaningfully. "Do you think one of them will get bored or fall out of love?"

Layla had the sense they were no longer talking about Aspen and Vera. "I don't know. But if they love each other enough…"

"Then?"

Her heart pounded. "Then they should be able to make

it work." Layla cleared her throat, her face hot. They needed to change the subject before she passed out. She forced a smile. "So what's the first thing you'll do when you get back to Japan?"

The rest of the dinner passed smoothly, discussing everything except the lingering question as to what they were doing. Will had confessed his love to her the other night, but they still skirted the issue of dating, and how they would manage a long-distance relationship.

After they ordered crème brûlée for dessert, they headed back to her dorm room. Aspen and Vera had also planned a romantic dinner tonight and would return to their hotel room, leaving Layla's dorm empty. Will grew silent as they approached her building. Layla tried to think of something to say, but the words died in her throat.

All too soon her dorm building loomed over them. Layla hesitated at the door. Will had his hands in his pocket.

"When does your flight leave again?"

"Tomorrow morning," Will said quietly.

"Right."

Will was silent, looking hard at the ground. Layla's heart sank. Was this it, then?

"I guess I'll—"

"Wait," Will said, his blue eyes loving and earnest. "I want to be with you, Layla. Even if I'm all the way in Japan for the next year. I'll make it work, I promise. I will get a job and save money so I can afford to fly here as often as I can. I don't care if it's crazy or difficult or stressful. I want it. I want you to be my girlfriend again."

Layla stared at him. She wanted to smile, to say his name, to say anything, but all she could do was stand frozen at his words, the words she had wanted him to say since the moment she saw his face appear on her phone and that love she had felt for him came rushing back all at once, paling the attraction she felt for Zach and occupying her every thought until she feared that she would go insane.

"But only if you want to," Will added quickly. "I totally understand if—"

He didn't finish the sentence, because Layla was already kissing him, her arms around his neck. Every word he spoke had only made her want to kiss him more and more until she couldn't hold herself back.

Will wrapped his arms around her waist and drew her in closer. Distantly she heard someone whistle at them, but the rest of the city marched on without a care that they kissed in the middle of the sidewalk. She brought her hands to Will's chest, which rose and fell rapidly beneath her touch.

"Come upstairs," she said breathlessly.

He looked at her with wide eyes, then nodded and kissed her again, as if he didn't have the words to answer. She pulled away and took his hand, guiding him towards the door. When they entered the elevator, Layla crowded him against the wall and kissed him. Then the elevator doors opened and they stumbled down the hall and to her room, pausing to kiss until she realized they were waiting for *her* to open the door. She could barely unlock the door without her hands shaking. Finally the door gave way and they kissed without breaking onto her bed, which she had thankfully remembered to make that morning.

She crawled on top of him and lifted her shirt off, then helped him take off his, revealing his pale golden torso, still toned from all those years playing lacrosse. Will looked up at her with those wide eyes, as if he had no idea how he had ended up in this position. Layla tried to unzip his pants but his hand on her arm stopped her.

"What?" Layla asked, her heart moving to her throat. Did he not want this?

Will hesitated. "I don't want you to think that I came here just for this."

Layla smirked. "Didn't you?"

"No," he said with a blush. "I mean, yes, I wanted to

kiss you. I have since the day I met you. But I don't want to rush anything. I know when we were still dating you wanted to wait…"

"I think I've waited long enough," Layla said dryly, then paused. "You know I've already…with Zach…"

Will half-smiled. "That's different. With me, it's new."

Layla felt her heart melt, and she leaned down and kissed him gently, hoping that the love she still felt for him passed through her kiss. "It is new. But I wouldn't want it any other way."

Then she guided his hands to the zipper of her skirt, which he drew down slowly, then helped her pull off. His skin was hot against hers as his arms wound around her waist, bringing her flush against him, closer than they had ever been before.

Will kissed her reverently in places she had never been kissed, and as the night drew to a close, Layla knew she had loved him all along.

17

Today was their last day in New York City. Aspen felt oddly relieved, even though she would miss Layla. Will had already left for Japan early in the morning. Layla's class ended at noon, so they agreed to meet in Central Park for a walk and then get lunch together.

Vera was already packed, her suitcase standing near the door. She poked her head out from the bathroom where she had just showered and looked at Aspen's clothes strewn across the floor.

"You haven't started packing?"

Aspen rolled her eyes. "Our flight isn't until tomorrow. I'll pack in the morning."

"Our flight is at *six* tomorrow morning," Vera said. "You should pack tonight."

"Worried I'll stay and never leave?" Aspen joked.

Vera stalked out of the bathroom in her towel, glaring at Aspen. "No. I'm worried we'll miss our flight because *someone* decided to pack last minute. You know we have to leave here by three-thirty in the morning at the latest?"

Aspen groaned. "Fine, I'll start packing." But she was smiling as she threw her clothes into her suitcase.

Once they were both ready, they took the subway north to Central Park. Layla was already waiting for them at one of the gated entrances. She looked the happiest Aspen had seen her since arriving, her face beaming as they hugged.

"Someone's happy," Aspen said, sharing a look with Vera. They both knew Will had spent the night at her place.

"Hey! Don't do that when I'm around," Layla said, crossing her arms.

Vera raised an amused brow. "Do what?"

"Talk about me when I'm right in front of you."

Aspen smirked. "But we didn't say anything."

"You didn't have to," Layla shot back.

Vera grabbed both their arms and dragged them inside the park. "It's our last day together. No fighting."

They grumbled but reluctantly agreed not to bicker anymore. Besides, the walk through the park was enchanting enough to distract them from their argument, the leaves of all the trees overhead exploding in various shades of red and orange, the last gasp of autumn before winter descended in full force. Children frolicked in the grass and played games while couples walked with their dogs or pushed strollers across the dirt paths.

It was a beautiful day, not too cold and not too hot. Aspen could envision herself taking walks in Central Park, then grabbing a bagel and coffee before heading to a shoot. Then she imagined herself living day in and day out alone, without Vera here holding her arm, and a part of her already felt lonely.

Once they walked past the lake and took photos on the bridge, Layla directed them to a popular sandwich shop and they ate lunch before Layla had to leave for her afternoon classes. But just as they were walking her to the nearest subway station, Aspen's phone rang.

She answered, and was greeted by the rich, accented voice of Miss Lavigne.

"Miss Aspen, good afternoon," Miss Lavigne said warmly. "Is this a good time?"

"Yes, yes, of course." Aspen moved away from Layla and Vera who stared at her with identical looks of alarm.

"I wanted to call you to inform you that we would love to welcome you to our agency," Miss Lavigne said. Aspen's heart dropped. "You may take a day or two to consider our offer, if you would like."

"No!" Aspen said quickly. "I mean, yes, I accept your offer. Thank you so much for the opportunity, I really appreciate it."

Miss Lavigne chuckled. "My team will email you soon with more information. I look forward to working with you, Miss Aspen."

They said goodbye and Aspen looked at Vera and Layla in silence.

"Well?" Layla asked anxiously.

Aspen couldn't help but smile, her eyes filling with tears. "I got accepted!"

Layla screamed and rushed forward to hug her. Aspen saw Vera smiling proudly. Once Layla let her go, Vera stepped forward and kissed her.

"I'm so proud of you," Vera whispered as she hugged her.

"We should celebrate!" Layla said. "I have class until five, but maybe we can get dinner together? Order a cake?"

"Come on guys, we don't have to make a big deal out of it," Aspen said.

Vera touched Aspen's cheek affectionately. "But it *is* a big deal. We're celebrating."

After dinner and cake, they said their final, teary goodbyes to Layla, who had to study for an exam and work on a project with another classmate.

But before they returned to their hotel for the night, Vera convinced Aspen to go to a bar, since Aspen had a very convincing fake ID and it wasn't every day they were in New York City together. The inside of the bar was dimly lit, with high-rise mahogany tables, booths, and a bar top with a wall of different alcoholic beverages behind it.

Aspen and Vera took a seat at one of the high-rise tables. They ordered their drinks—a gin and tonic for Vera and a Cosmopolitan for Aspen—then sat for a few minutes enjoying the soft, lilting jazz and quiet conversation that filled the room.

"I don't think we've ever traveled together," Vera said, taking Aspen's hand on the table.

"If you don't count that time in high school when I joined your family vacation to Palm Springs."

Vera half-smiled. "I don't."

"Well, that was the first time I realized that I liked girls," Aspen confessed, remembering that time sitting by the pool and seeing Vera in a bikini. All day long she had pretended to squint at the sun just to sneak looks at Vera instead.

"Really?"

"You always forget how hot you are," Aspen said, shaking her head.

Vera blushed. "You're the only person who thinks I'm hot."

"Not true! I'm just the only person brave enough to make a move on *the* Vera Wyer."

"Well, one day we should travel together," Vera said. "Just the two of us."

Aspen's belly fluttered with excitement at the thought. "To where?"

"I always wanted to go to London."

"Me too," Aspen agreed. She lifted Vera's hand and kissed her knuckles. "One day I'll take you there. I promise."

Vera's eyes shined. "I know."

"Do you think…do you think one day you could see us…maybe…getting married?"

The words left Aspen's mouth before she could stop them, but she didn't regret asking them. They had been on her mind for some time now.

Instead of the shock she expected to find, Vera merely smiled. "I wouldn't be with you if I didn't."

Instantly Aspen's heart flooded with warmth. "I can't afford a ring yet, but when I can we'll get married. There's no one in this world I want to be with besides you."

Vera's eyes filled with tears. "Even if we're apart for the next ten years, I only want you."

Aspen leaned over the table and kissed her, their hands holding each other tightly between them, as if they were both afraid to let go.

When they leaned back, Vera raised her glass, her cheeks glistening with tears. "To the future."

"To us," Aspen whispered, clinking their glasses.

Soon they returned to their hotel and went to sleep after Aspen finished packing her bags for their flight early the next morning. As they boarded the plane together, still bleary-eyed from a lack of sleep, Aspen knew that even if they were a world apart, they would always find their way back to each other.

In a few weeks, she would be in New York City, where the future glimmered in all its vast uncertainty, but for the present, Aspen had hope once more, and that was enough.

Epilogue

SIX YEARS LATER

"**D**oes Aspen seem... off to you?" Vera asked, taking a sip of her coffee and trying to seem nonchalant. Layla didn't buy it. They had met up for coffee, after all, which was always code for relationship problems.

"What do you mean? Like 'she's feeling sick' off, or…" Layla said, sounding worried.

They both knew what the *or* meant, especially Layla, who had been through multiple breakups throughout high school and college, and after she and Will broke up three years ago, she had been on and off dating apps, where she met her current British lawyer boyfriend.

But Vera didn't want to think that *or* applied to her and Aspen. Sure, they have had their fair share of fights over the past nine years, including their year apart when

Vera first went to college and their near break up a year or so later. That was all in the past though, and for the last few years living in New York together, where Vera studied for her PhD and Aspen continued to model, their relationship had only gotten stronger. So why was Vera doubting them?

"I don't know," Vera said. "She's been sort of distant lately."

It was true enough. For the past few months, Aspen had grown quiet. Several times, Vera had spotted Aspen hunched over her laptop typing away, but whenever Vera got closer to take a look, Aspen would quickly shut the laptop and mutter some excuse. Not only that, but she had started working overtime, booking extra shoots, taking on other jobs, even ones that would take her out of town for days at a time. It seemed like Vera rarely saw Aspen these days.

"Have you talked to her about it?" Layla asked. This was a line that Vera usually used on Layla whenever she came to her about boy troubles. Vera found that she didn't quite like being on the receiving end of it.

"Of course not," Vera said with a scowl, feeling seventeen instead of twenty-six. "She'd think I'm doubting her or something. And what if I'm just being paranoid?"

"*Are* you being paranoid?" Layla asked slowly, raising

a brow. Again, it was something Vera would probably say.

"I don't know! That's why I'm asking you if Aspen is being weird. She's your best friend, you should know," Vera said.

Layla rolled her eyes. "Aspen has been and always will be a complete mystery to me. But I do know that she loves you. A lot. I don't know why she's acting distant, but I'm sure she has a good reason."

Vera bit her lip before asking her next question. She hadn't wanted to consider it, but she'd regret it if she didn't at least ask it aloud. "You don't think Aspen's... cheating, do you?"

Layla's eyes widened. "What? No! Of course not. I mean, you don't really think that, right? She wouldn't do that to you."

"No, but…" Vera kept her eyes trained on her coffee cup. Of course Aspen wouldn't cheat on her. But wasn't that what everyone said about the person they loved?

"Give it a week or so," Layla said, "and if she's still like this, then you have to talk to her."

"Fine," Vera said, dread already curling in her stomach at the thought. "Two weeks."

Two weeks passed, then three, then four, and soon summer was fast approaching. Aspen continued to keep her distance. Vera stayed silent.

"I mean, you have to talk to her," Will said, his face blurring on her phone screen when the reception failed. He was currently in Africa somewhere, helping out small communities by building schools and public restrooms.

"I know," Vera said with a sigh, "but how? She's not even in New York right now. She's working in San Francisco for a week." Or at least, that's what Aspen had told her. She could be doing anything right now.

"When she comes back, talk to her," Will said. Then they changed the subject to Will's travels in Africa and Vera's continued study of aerospace engineering and how she had secured an internship at NASA for July before they said their goodbyes.

After talking with Will, Vera felt like she needed to consult someone a little closer to home. She decided to go visit her parents for a week while Aspen was away, since she still had some airline credits and her summer break had just started. Besides, she hadn't seen her parents since January. Vera wasn't usually so spontaneous, but she felt nervous about the situation.

She texted her mom that she was visiting and didn't wait for a reply before booking an early flight for the next morning. From the airport, Vera ordered a ride to her childhood home. It looked the same as it always had, and for a moment Vera felt like that young girl again driving back home from school, eager to get started on her *Grapes of Wrath* essay. Little did Vera's younger self know that that night would change her life forever.

She walked to the door and rang the doorbell. Vera had a key, but she felt awkward suddenly barging in, feeling more like a visitor and not someone who had lived there for nearly nineteen years.

The door swung open and her mother's face appeared.

"Vera! This was very last minute. I didn't have time to clean up," she said, but she was smiling as she hugged Vera.

"Don't worry, Mom," Vera said with a laugh. "I'm sure by my standards the house is very clean."

Her mom sighed, smiling sadly as she stepped away. "God, I've missed you." She discreetly wiped a tear from her cheek, before they both headed inside.

"I've missed you too," Vera said with a sigh.

"But is something wrong?" her mom asked as she took out some snacks for Vera to eat.

Vera hesitated. Now that she was here, she realized it was hard to put into words. "Well, you see, for the past few months, nothing's wrong—yet, at least—that I know of, but, well…"

Her mother raised a brow. "Is it Aspen?"

"How did you know?" Vera asked with a nervous smile.

"Oh sweetie, it's my job to know," her mother said, and her comforting smile and teasing tone helped soothe Vera's anxiety.

"But it could have been Layla," Vera said pointedly.

"If it was Layla, I would've heard from her first. Immediately."

Vera laughed despite her nerves. "That's true." She never had been good at expressing her emotions.

"Well, what's going on with Aspen? Did you guys get in a fight?"

"Not exactly," Vera said, clasping her hands together in an attempt to stop them from trembling. She hadn't realized how close to tears she was until her mother embraced her.

"Just tell me everything," her mother said, the palm of her hand rubbing soothing circles on her back.

Vera did.

When Vera returned to her apartment a week later, the

days had grown even more humid, and she dreaded the stifling heat of her apartment that would surely be empty.

But when she arrived at the apartment it was cold, as if the air conditioning had been running. *Weird.* She didn't remember leaving it on before she left. But Aspen wasn't supposed to return until tomorrow. Her heart pounded in her chest.

Could it be…? No, it couldn't—

"Vera?" —

It was. Before Vera found the courage to move, Aspen emerged from their bedroom, dressed in sweats and one of Vera's UCLA sweatshirts, looking as beautiful as ever.

"Aspen? What are you doing here?" Vera asked in disbelief. Aspen laughed, a sound Vera thought she must not have heard for a few weeks now.

"What do you mean? I live here. And I finished work a day early. Where were—wait, were you traveling?" Aspen stopped in her tracks, looking at Vera's carry-on suitcase. She took a few steps towards her, her eyes widening. "Have you been crying?"

No, I'm fine, was on the tip of Vera's tongue, but miraculously, she held the words back. She recalled what her mother had told her as she cried in her arms. *Both of you deserve the truth.*

"Yes," Vera said, her voice barely a whisper. Surprise

and worry blossomed across Aspen's face. "I was visiting my parents for the week while you were gone."

"Why didn't you tell me? What's wrong? Did something happen? Your parents? Layla?" Aspen looked tense, possibly because she knew what it felt like to be on the receiving end of bad news.

"No, my parents are fine. And so is Layla," Vera said, and Aspen relaxed momentarily before anxiously searching Vera's face, as if she might find the answer hidden there.

"Then why were you crying?" Aspen asked. "Your studies?"

"No, that's fine—"

"Is it Will?" Aspen interrupted. "Did something happen in Africa?"

"No—"

But Aspen cut her off again. "Are you okay? Did you go to the doctor?"

"Aspen, I'm fine, at least health-wise. This has nothing to do with that," Vera said, starting to lose her patience. She understood why Aspen was getting slightly hysterical because of her experiences in the past with her dad, but at some point she would need to listen.

"Then what—"

"It's you, okay?" Vera said, and Aspen fell silent, her

mouth parted in shock. "I mean, you've been so distant lately. At first, I thought it was nothing, maybe something happened at work or you just needed space. But after a few weeks…and then months…"

Aspen stared at Vera for a full three seconds, blinking slowly, before she groaned and covered her face with her hands.

"I'm so sorry, I didn't even realize!" Aspen exclaimed.

Vera felt her confusion fade into anxiety. "What?"

"Oh wow, I'm such a terrible girlfriend," Aspen said, almost laughing. "I've been so caught up with it that I forgot you wouldn't understand what I was doing."

Vera's anxiety quickly transformed into annoyance. "Aspen, can you please tell me what's going on."

Aspen looked at Vera in surprise and…nervousness? "Yeah, sure, but hold on." She quickly disappeared to their room and then came back, holding a thin folder in her hands.

"What's this about, Aspen?" Vera asked, her anxiousness returning swiftly at the sight of the strange folder.

"So, you obviously have noticed that I've been working more," Aspen said. Vera nodded. "It's because I've been trying to save some money."

Vera looked up at Aspen's face in shock. Aspen's eyes were wide and bright, as if she were showing her a project she had worked really hard on.

"For what?"

Aspen bit her lip, then held out the file. Vera cautiously walked over and took it.

"I'm scared," Vera said, the most honest she had been in months.

Instead of the *don't be* she was expecting, all Aspen said was, "Open it."

Vera carefully opened the folder to a printed page. She saw letters. Numbers. A blue background. Ads on the side. A small plane icon.

"You bought plane tickets."

"To London."

"To London?" Vera repeated, her voice weak. She didn't know what to say. This was what Aspen had been hiding behind her back? And all this time she had been wondering if Aspen was cheating on her. She felt awful, but her heart soared. She had always wanted to visit London.

"I'm a horrible person," Vera said, and Aspen opened her mouth to speak. "No, Aspen, you don't understand. I thought you were cheating on me. Instead you were doing this!"

Aspen smiled softly. "You're not a horrible person. You felt how anyone would feel if their girlfriend was stupid enough to be so obvious about a surprise trip like this. I didn't realize how bad it looked until now."

"I can't believe it," Vera said, unable to fight back a smile. She was going to London!

Before Aspen could speak, Vera threw her arms around her and pulled her into a tight hug. Aspen leaned back only enough to kiss Vera, intermingled with a mess of *sorry*'s and *I love you*'s and excited laughs.

Aspen lifted Vera with the idea of carrying her to their bed, but Vera swatted at her arms. "Put me down! I'll drop the papers."

"They're just papers, Vera," Aspen said with a smile. "Kiss me."

Vera didn't need to be told twice.

"I think I'll get the truffle pasta," Aspen said absentmindedly, flipping the laminated menu over to the alcohol section. "And a bottle of the Cabernet."

Vera ordered the steak. Once the waiter left she looked over the railing beside their table, soaking up the London skyline. "It's a lovely view."

"I had to get reservations months ago," Aspen said, staring out over the restaurant balcony at the Thames

River, glittering with the lights of the city.

"Thank you for this," Vera said. "It means so much to me that you planned everything."

Sometimes Vera felt like she hadn't said it enough. The trip had been incredible so far, visiting the beautiful wonders of London that Vera had always dreamed of seeing in real life, and at the day's end returning to a five-star, luxury hotel with the softest sheets Vera had ever felt. And they still planned to visit the English countryside for a few days.

Aspen took Vera's hand in hers. "I'd do it a million times just to see that smile on your face."

Vera blushed and was saved from trying to come up with a response when their waiter announced his presence and served them their appetizers.

The dinner passed like a dream. As with everything else since they arrived in London, the food and wine were amazing, and when the waiter asked if they would like the dessert menus, Vera couldn't resist saying yes. Now they stood looking out over London, gazing at the enchanting cityscape.

"That was…" Vera had no words. She gripped the railings as if to make sure it was all real.

Aspen leaned in close, covering Vera's hand with hers. They looked up at the dark sky, pierced by the illuminated Big Ben that seemed to watch over the city.

"Awesome? Spectacular? Sexy?" Aspen suggested.

Vera huffed a laugh. "Sexy? How can dinner be sexy? Actually, don't answer that."

Aspen laughed, a melody Vera could hear for hours on end. "I thought feeding each other warm, melted, dripping chocolate cake was pretty sexy."

"Okay, okay, I see your point." Vera couldn't stop blushing, and even though she'd felt like this many times while they'd been together, flushed and excited, it never ceased to feel electric and new each time.

"Can you believe this?" Aspen asked, her voice full of wonder, her eyes searching the horizon like she was trying to drink up everything in sight.

Vera shook her head. "That I'd be dating a model, who is also the most amazing person I know, on a trip to London, my favorite city in the world? No, it's really hard to believe."

Aspen squeezed her hand. "Sometimes I wonder what would've happened if I never got drunk that night. If I never showed up at your door."

Vera closed her eyes, remembering Aspen swaying on her doorstep as though it were yesterday, her long legs in high heels and her black, silky hair falling over her shoulder.

"Vera," Aspen said.

Vera turned, and Aspen was facing her, all teasing laughter from before gone.

Aspen's eyes shined, and she looked truly happy despite the somber aura that seemed to hover around them. "I wouldn't want to be alive if that night never happened. If *we* never happened."

"Me too," Vera said softly.

"Every moment with you is like falling. Falling and then flying, with every smile, with every laugh, with every kiss. Every day I fall more in love with you than before, even more than I could imagine. You helped me in my moments of despair and weakness, when I could barely stand the thought of another day, and through your love you helped show me the way to a light and beauty that I had never felt or known before. A life without you would be no life at all."

Aspen stepped away and lowered down to one knee, pulling out a small black box. Vera's heart pounded so loud everyone in London must have heard it. She could barely breathe, her eyes locked onto the box in Aspen's elegant fingers.

"Vera Evelyn Wyer," Aspen said, a slight tremor in her voice. She opened the box, displaying a ring inset with a small, glowing diamond. "Will you marry me?"

Vera's eyes filled with tears, and she swore that her body was floating. "Yes, of course, yes! I love you. Yes!"

Aspen slipped the ring on Vera's finger with shaky hands, then stood up and kissed her.

A sudden gust of wind whipped through Vera's hair as they kissed, and in that moment, wrapped up in Aspen's embrace and as light as a bird darting through the sky, Vera felt like she was truly flying.

Acknowledgements

First, I would like to acknowledge all the readers who supported my debut novel and the first book of this series, *My Sister's Best Friend,* whether on Wattpad or through Amazon. The tremendous support I have felt from family, friends, and readers alike has given me the confidence to publish this sequel, as well as continue my writing career.

Best Friends & Their Exes was developed from a bonus chapter I had written online for the first free version of *MSBF*. Since then, not only has the story grown in the telling, but so have I as a person. I hope everyone who read the first book could grow with the characters as they aged and matured along with their author, and that the message of their story still gives hope to those who believe in love.

I would like to personally thank my talented cousin and graphic designer, Alexis, who made the new covers of both *MSBF* and *BFTE*. Her artistry has given the series a more cohesive, elevated look that I felt was needed for the new editions. As always, thank you to my family and friends who have supported my writing journey since the start, and even before then. Your encouragement and belief in me keeps me writing every day.

About the Author

Zoë Tavares Bennett is a writer based in Los Angeles, California. She is also the author of the Ancient Mediterranean inspired fantasy novel, *The Song of Gaia,* as well as the historical novel *The Sun of God*. She has a degree in Classics from Williams College, specializing in Ancient Greek and Latin.